Murder Strikes the Set

A Simmons Pettigru Mystery

Linda Shirley Robertson

FpS

Greenville, South Carolina

Murder Strikes the Set

by Linda Shirley Robertson

ISBN: 978-1-952248-61-0 (trade paperback)

Published by:

FpS

1175 Woods Crossing Rd., #2
Greenville, S.C. 29607
864-675-0540
www.fiction-addiction.com

Cover & Book Design
by United Writers Press

Printed in the United States of America.

Murder Strikes the Set *was written for readers who want to put on cozy clothes, grab a cup of their favorite cozy liquid, and curl up with Simmons Pettigru as she sleuths into murder on a set of the "Scottish Play."*

1

The Piedmont hills buzzed with the sound of mosquitoes. Some of these pests are bigger and more bothersome than ants at a picnic. I swatted at the swarm around my face as I opened the door of my Volvo.

I moved back to my hometown of Rosemont, S.C. a couple of weeks ago with the plan to sell the family home that I had inherited. We did not have swarms of pests in New York City—although a few of my friends claimed that they could tame the rats that ran through the halls of their apartments.

It was late afternoon on that August day in Rosemont. I locked the car and made my way up the path to the door of my family home, McBee Mansion.

I felt the sizzle of the pavement beneath the soles of my espadrilles. Dark thunderclouds scuttled across the sun and a crop of chill bumps danced along my arms.

McBee Mansion had a reputation of being haunted. Aunt Stacy, my closest living relative, had once told me the story of Alfred Redfern, who had fallen down the front hall stairs and broken his neck. Rumor had it he had threatened to expose a poker game that the McBees held every week and claimed he'd been cheated out of a sizable amount of money.

I had personally never seen a ghost in the house, but my mother claimed that a young girl often walked along the steps to the third floor. The girl and her mother had allegedly been killed during an Indian raid when a log cabin stood on the site. When great Uncle Hugh McBee and his brother, who was my great-grandfather, built the place, the ghosts reportedly settled into the foundation of my family's home. Or what *used* to be the old homeplace.

The sole direct survivor of Rosemont's founding family, I no longer wanted a mansion—instead, I wanted to get rid of the burden and get on with my life. Hired as the new artistic director of the Rhett Street Players, I had come back home to fulfill my lifelong desire to write and direct a play.

I felt oddly unsettled as I walked down the hall toward voices at the other end. A memory pierced my brain—my grandfather holding his arms open and me running like a flying spear toward him. I shook off the image—the loud voices I heard, after all, weren't coming from my head. They were coming from the dining room.

Members of the Rhett Street Board Theater Group were seated around a large conference table. I took a seat by Kate Mason, my best friend from childhood, and looked around. I'd been gone from Rosemont a while but some of the people still seemed familiar.

Kate stood and started the meeting. "We are here today to finalize plans for our upcoming fundraiser." She turned and pointed to me. "This is our new director, Simmons Pettigru. Since our theater troupe needs a new home, I want this to be the most successful fundraiser that Rosemont has ever seen. We would love to raise enough money to find a permanent home. I have asked Simmons to share her new ideas for a fundraiser that will bring in a lot of money for us." Kate looked at me and smiled.

The board members didn't all seem to be pleased with this announcement and everyone began to talk at once. Kate banged the gavel on the table—which must have been at least a hundred years old. I cringed at the thought that it was probably the original dining table Nana insisted be shipped from France in the early 1800s, but I kept a smile plastered on my face. The table would probably survive another century, but it didn't sound like the board would be around much longer. Myrtle Meyers seemed to be the most vocal.

"How can you possibly say that my idea for a garden party won't raise the money we need? Simmons, tell Kate that your great-grandfather built this place for parties. Have you all seen the ballroom on the third floor? It is magnificent and ready for a soirée!"

Before I could respond, Kate jumped into the fray and got everyone to stop talking. I tried to give her the best stink eye I could manage but she wasn't looking at me. The rest of the board members, however, *were*.

I took a deep breath and stood up. "Before I start, it might be helpful for each of you to introduce yourselves. Coming back to Rosemont has been a blessing for me. As you know, I have been in New York for the past ten years and my memory isn't so good."

Kate jumped up and started the introductions. "Margaret Sellers and Maddie Taylor—they are in charge of decorations and refreshments." The ladies put their hands in the air. "Eric Loftis is a commercial developer who will be in charge of ticket sales." A man near the end of the table raised his hand.

The only other male at the table looked up. "I'm Jackson Williams," he said. "I will be the coordinator between the chamber and the board. I own a little realty company too and will be able to get a lot of ticket sales from my clients and my Rosemont Chamber of Commerce friends." Kate gave him a big smile. I had been back just long enough to know some of what was going on in town. He must be Kate's significant other, I thought.

"I think you know Myrtle," said Kate. "She is in charge of entertainment and—"

Myrtle stood up and loudly announced that she had been placed in charge of a lovely tea and garden party for the fundraiser and that if that didn't happen, she just might not help.

Kate continued talking without losing a beat. "Simmons, I know you have met Sally Goldman. She owns the Mark and Goldman Ad Agency. She has volunteered to help us advertise our party. We will all, of course, be selling tickets." She gestured toward the first two women again. "Oh, and I forgot. Margaret and Maddie are the sustainers from the Junior League."

Kate pushed a strand of her curly blonde hair out of her eyes. "Simmons, would you please share your idea for our fundraiser? This will be a sure way for us to raise more than enough for a downpayment on a new home." She motioned for me to continue.

Tension permeated the room—thick enough to stab with a dagger from the "Scottish Play," which was apropos since I felt as if I was auditioning for a part in Shakespeare's tragedy. "Let me give you the backstory. I hope when I'm finished that you will understand why Kate thought that this would be a great way to raise money for the Rhett Street Players."

Everyone quieted down somewhat and I began again. "A few years ago I played Lady Macbeth in summer stock with an actor and producer named Max Everhart. He went on to win a Tony for a Broadway play that he produced and directed called *Bridge Across the Sky*. It had a great run on Forty Second Street."

I cleared my throat. The board was still staring at me. I detected what I thought was a twinkle in Eric Loftis's blue eyes—a simmering contrast to his black wavy hair. I took a sip of water and forged ahead. "When my husband died about a year ago, I decided to move back to Rosemont. The lights of Broadway no longer had much appeal for me. Max and I remain friends—we've stayed in touch.

"First, I am delighted to be your new artistic director. I have asked Max and his wife, Veronica, to perform a few scenes of the Scottish Play as part of the fundraiser. They are flying from New York to the Greenville-Spartanburg Airport, as we speak, to meet you." I looked at my watch. "In fact, they should be here any minute."

About that moment, I heard a loud rumble. I knew it wasn't my stomach—I had had a great lunch with my Aunt Stacy at Tipsy Taco. I looked out the window. The bright sunlight was now hidden behind large black storm clouds. I felt chill bumps run down my back again.

"How will Shakespeare scenes fit in with my garden party?" asked Myrtle. "Besides, Simmons, your dear departed family would not be happy that you plan to bring actors into this lovely home that has stood for as long as Rosemont has existed. This is a respectable neighborhood and this type of fundraiser could lead to outsiders moving in or a development company turning it into an apartment complex." She turned to Kate. "I thought we were going to partner with the Carolina Garden Club and use it as a meeting place for respectable clubs. Isn't that what you told me?"

Everyone started shouting at each other and Kate banged the gavel again. "Yes, Myrtle, that was our original thought. But Simmons has already had several proposals and I think even an offer for this property. Eric, would you speak to this matter?"

Eric stood and adjusted his bowtie—a bright turquoise that matched the print in his shirt. I smiled at him and sat down. He looked good enough to be on the cover of *GQ*.

"It is true," he said, "that Simmons had several offers even before she came back from New York. One offer was from a company that planned to raze the house and build condo units."

"Over my dead body!" Myrtle screamed.

"I second that motion," Maddie hollered.

Kate's voice rose above the den but was drowned out by a large clap of thunder. "Maddie, there is no motion on the floor to second. Please let Simmons finish her presentation and then we can take turns talking through our concerns."

I looked around the table again. The board was a diverse group. There was a mixed bag of ages…and opinions. As director of the theater, I'll have to answer to this board, I thought. It didn't seem to be a cohesive agreeable group. I was instantly glad I hadn't said that out loud.

I cleared my throat and started again. "First of all, I have accepted no offers at this time. In the meantime, Max and Veronica have agreed to do a few scenes from the Scottish Play as part of the fundraiser. I think it is a lovely idea to have wine and cheese in the garden before the performance. We could charge a lot more for people in Rosemont to meet and watch Broadway stars. Perhaps some friends from other towns would come."

I paused for a moment. "In anticipation of their doing the scenes, I asked that a set for the Scottish Play be built on the third floor stage. I know it's a lot to work out, but Max and Veronica said they wanted to stop by here this afternoon and get a feel for it. When we're done here, I'm inviting you all to go up to the third floor with me and see what it looks like. I ask only that you give my idea fair consideration."

I sat down and looked around the table.

"What *is* this Scottish Play?" Myrtle asked. "It's not some rock and roll rap stuff, is it?"

I jumped back up. Things might get out of hand if Kate and I let the board members continue to control the meeting. "It is one of the best plays ever written," I said. "Shakespeare wrote it between 1599 and 1606. The play was originally called the *Tragedy of Macbeth,* which I'm sure you've all heard of, but from the beginning there's been a curse on it. When the play is presented on stage and an actor says the name Macbeth out of context, dire things happen."

I looked around the table again. "For instance, the last time Max and Veronica performed the show, an usher broke his leg and a witch's cauldron tipped over and dropped dry ice on a woman. No one admitted that they had said the king's name, but we knew someone had. I don't plan to say it out of context either—although we will do a few scenes from the play."

I signaled for Kate to take over again and moved to sit down but before I was back in my chair, lightning danced around the garden and a loud clap of thunder roared in our ears. The room was suddenly bathed in an inky darkness. Chairs scraped and the sound of people moving in different directions was heard.

"Where is the fuse box?" asked Kate's friend Jackson. "I hope it's inside. The skies have opened up. Do you hear it? I can't believe the downpour. I don't want to go outside."

I felt my way around the table and headed for the kitchen. I hoped there were candles or maybe a flashlight in a drawer. I stepped on a lump of soft flesh but it didn't move. *Who said not over my dead body?* I bent down and there was Myrtle huddled in a ball near the kitchen door.

I grabbed her wrist to feel for a pulse. "Are you okay?"

"I'm okay," she whispered. "The first clap of thunder was actually thunder. The second clap was me going under the table. I am deathly afraid of storms."

I breathed a sigh of relief. A lot of women like Myrtle, who looked to be well over sixty-five, were afraid of being struck by lightning.

In the kitchen junk drawer, I found a flashlight with some battery power and headed up the back steps. I heard footsteps behind me and turned around. It was Jackson. "I am on my way to see if the fuse box is on the third floor," he said.

When we reached the top of the stairs, we turned the corner and entered the ballroom. I looked toward the stage and stopped cold, causing Jackson to bump into me. Beside the frame around the stage, or the *proscenium* as we call it in the business, I could make out something shiny.

But before I could get to it, my flashlight dimmed. I took a step, expecting Jackson to follow, but he touched my arm. "Let's go back downstairs and I'll call Duke Energy on my cell phone," he said. "Power could be out in all the houses in this area if the lightning struck a power pole. We could get hurt up here. The set designers could have left tools in here. Here, take my hand and I'll get us back to the door and down the steps."

I pushed my hand into his but before we could reach the door, every fixture that my family had ever installed in this old mansion burst into bright light. I turned to see what I hope never to see again. A man was lying on the floor with a dagger protruding from his back.

Max Everhart.

2

I wobbled down the front steps of McBee Mansion and took a deep breath, filling my lungs with fresh rain-soaked air. My legs shook like key lime Jello in a parfait glass.

It would be a long time before I could rid myself of the sight of Max's blood pooling on the floor and the blotch on his blue polo shirt. The dagger had obviously been real—not the fake that would be used in the play.

I covered my face with my hands and almost screamed when the front door opened. Bill Randolph, a man who had once been my high school sweetheart, walked down the steps and sat next to me. I looked at him in confusion.

"Bill? Is it really you? You're the detective that caught this case? I thought you were practicing law with your father."

He shook his head. "I thought you were working in New York City."

"I was. I used to be the stage manager for the Forty-Second Street Theater. My husband was an investment banker on Wall Street. He died last winter in a skiing accident in Switzerland and my Aunt Stacy convinced me to come back to Rosemont and take

10

some time off. When Uncle Hugh died, I inherited this place. I was going to put it on the market after the theater fundraiser, but now…" Tears pooled in my eyes and I tried to wipe my face with the sleeve of my blouse.

Bill leaned in. "I have a few questions for you. Sorry they can't wait until tomorrow."

I shrugged. "I would rather talk now anyway," I said, wiping at my face again. "I have no idea who would want to kill Max. He didn't know anyone in Rosemont."

"Why was he here?"

"I read in the *Actor's Weekly News* that he and his wife were going to Highlands, NC to see his sister May and got in touch with him to see if he and Veronica would help with our fundraiser."

Bill said nothing so I continued. "I can't believe another murder has happened here. Grandfather and Uncle Hugh once told me the story of one that occurred here in 1937. Someone pushed Alfred Redfern down the front hall stairs, but that murder was never solved. My great Aunt Louise always said it was the little girl ghost that lives in the attic and walks up and down the stairs at night. I don't know if you have heard those tales. How will I ever sell this property with all the blood that has been spilled here?"

"Tell me everything that you remember after the lights went out. I need to compare your story with the theater board members when I interview them."

I realized that I couldn't be certain where most of the board members had been. *Could one of them have done it?*

"Will you question the set builders who were upstairs during our meeting? I think I heard some hammering."

"I have their names and will track them down tomorrow. But first, I have a lot of questions for some of the board members."

I felt a tear run down my cheek. I didn't want to believe that anyone on the board could be a killer.

Bill took a few more notes and stood up. I tried to stand with him but my legs were still weak. The wind whipped around the corner of the house and the bun on the back of my head came undone. I pushed long wet hair out of my eyes and grabbed the hand rail.

"If I need to get in touch, are you staying here?" asked Bill.

"No. Until I find the right condo to buy, I will be at the Rosemont Inn."

"I hope your plans work out. I would love to catch up with you once I have solved the case." He turned and went back into the dark interior of the house.

Catch up? What did he mean by that? He was probably married and had a bunch of kids. Besides, this was certainly not the time to think about my future life in Rosemont. I needed to take one day at a time.

It was time for me to go back to the Inn, but I needed to find Veronica. Hadn't she been with Max? I shook the cobwebs from my head. The thought of Veronica as a killer was ludicrous.

I assumed that someone had already told her what had happened and I needed to make sure she was okay. "Put on your big girl pants," I said to myself, and started toward my Volvo.

A movement behind the boxwoods caught my eye. A fat calico kitten scampered around the corner of the house and let out a huge meow. Just as I reached down to pet the kitten, I noticed a brown leather wallet and picked it up. Eric Loftis barreled around the corner from the back of the house. "Thank goodness," he said. "You found my wallet. It fell out of my pocket when I was looking for the fuse box." He grabbed the wallet from my hands and looked through it. "Thank goodness I don't have to replace everything."

Just as Eric turned to go, the kitten charged out of the bushes and latched onto his pant leg. He tried to shake it off and then leaned down to grab it by its head. I realized he was planning to throw the kitten across the yard and screamed. Eric lost his balance and fell into the bushes, and the cat jumped away.

"I have called the vet several times about that damn cat," he said, redfaced. "Its owners moved and left the cat to roam the neighborhood. It is a nuisance and if I ever catch it, I will send it to the Humane Society."

I looked down at the cat, which was now rubbing against my leg. It looked a lot like the calico my brother had named Awesome Wasome when we were kids. After Bill went off to college, Awesome slept on my head. I scooped the cat up in my arms and it settled down and purred. Instantly, I knew it had to be mine.

Eric shook his head and walked away. "Please get rid of that cat," he called back to me. I ignored him.

"Well," I said, stroking its fur, "if I'm going to keep you, you need a checkup and a new name. I'm going to take you to the vet in Rosemont Park, and I can't just call you Cat."

The streets weren't crowded and it only took a few minutes to get to the Rosemont Animal Clinic. I picked up the cat and headed to the clinic door. Another familiar figure was locking the door as I ran up the steps. "Wait," I yelled. "I need to get this cat checked out. I want to adopt it." I caught my breath and looked straight into the eyes of Jim Allen, another old friend from high school days.

"Why, Simmons McBee," he said. "I heard you were back in town. Are you back for good?" He glanced down at the movement in my arms. "Looks like you found the cat that the Joneses left behind when they moved to Pittsburgh. Its owner told me to find it a good home if I could catch it. I thought Eric would have taken it to the shelter by now."

"Yes, I'm back. I hope to sell Uncle Hugh's house and find a condo or a small house to buy. I am the new director of the Rhett Street Players." I handed the cat to him. "How is Margo? Are you all still living on Longview Terrace?"

Jim took the little Cat in and put him on the examining table. He seemed to be ignoring my question. After giving Cat a thorough exam he gave me a thumbs up and started filling out a chart. "Name?" he said.

"Simmons *Pettigru*. I married Michael Pettigru. He was in the class ahead of us."

Jim looked at me and laughed out loud.

"Why is that funny? Don't you remember that I married Michael while we were in college and—" I stopped and giggled. He wanted the name of the cat.

I had given some thought to it on the way over. I looked at the bright-eyed furry ball and announced that his name would be Max, in tribute to my friend.

"Simmons, I'm afraid it'll have to be Max*ine*." I blushed when I thought about it. Of course, Max was a she. *All* calico cats are.

I looked at my new calico furbaby. "Let's make it Maxie instead."

While I reached in my purse for a credit card, Jim opened the door to a storage room and pulled out a cat bed, food, and a litter box. When the transaction was finished, I grabbed the supplies and my credit card receipt. Maxie and I were ready to load the car.

Jim carried the supplies and helped me get everything into the backseat of the Volvo. Maxie immediately hopped into the cat bed and made herself comfortable. I started the car and put it in reverse. Jim tapped on the window and I let it down.

"Margo and I are divorced—almost two years now. I'm seeing Joan, the woman who owns the Rosemont Inn." He gently drummed his fingers on the door and smiled as he walked away.

I had known Joan since her family moved to Rosemont. We'd sat next to each other in second grade and become instant friends. I remembered the night in tenth grade when we tried to dye our curly brown tresses blonde and they'd turned our hair orange.

I was an only child and, although she had two older brothers, Joan was the only girl child. We had always been there for each other. In some ways, we were closer than sisters. She and Kate had come all the way to New York for Michael's memorial service.

A cool breeze blew in through the window as I backed up and pulled onto the road. Breezes were rare for summer in Rosemont— and I left the window down on the drive back to the Inn. Maxie didn't even stir.

When I turned into the parking lot, only one other car was there—and it belonged to Joan. Where was Veronica? Could *she* have killed Max? No, I thought, that was absurd. She and Max had a great relationship.

I shook my head—too much had happened in the course of the day. I would deal with those thoughts later.

As I reached for Maxie, a car pulled up beside me. It was Bill.

"Let me help you," he said. "I came over to see if I could talk to Veronica. Joan is on the desk tonight and I usually eat here on Wednesdays. They have the best crab cakes in town. Care to join me?"

"Is it still Wednesday?" I said. Bill smiled and nodded, and I shook my head. "It has been a long day. Crab cakes sound great. I'll put Maxie in my room and be right back." I looked down at my new pet and paused. "I guess Joan won't mind if I have a cat." It was the first time I'd even thought about it.

"I expect it will be okay," said Bill. "I'll bet her dog Britt is under the desk. That dog *loves* to greet the guests."

3

It took a few minutes for me to get the cat bed and litter box set up—the room was too small for both me and a cat.

An 11x14 oriental rug covered most of the room. Generic prints of flowers hung on the walls. The bedspread was a light blue. It would show cat hairs if Maxie decided she wanted to sleep with me. I would have to put Maxie's litter box in the bathroom, which was the size of a small closet in the mansion.

I put food in a bowl and water on the rug beside a mahogany night stand and looked at my new companion. "Okay, Maxie, you are settled. This is our home for now." I glanced at myself in the mirror and closed the door behind me. I was definitely back in the South—I was a widow and was talking to a cat.

Bill was standing by the desk with a frown on his face.

"What's wrong?" I asked.

"Neither Veronica nor Max ever checked in," said Joan. "And they didn't cancel their reservations."

I looked at Bill and then back at Joan. "What do you think happened? Do you think they never meant to stay here? I can't believe that they wouldn't have called."

"I don't know," she said. "I told Bill that I would call him if Veronica showed up." She paused. "Enjoy your meal. Our new chef is on fire. His food is James-Beard delicious." I looked down at my watch—although it was now past dinnertime, Joan had kept the food hot for us. She gave me a quick wink. *Did she seriously think I was interested in Bill?* Before today, I hadn't seen him in years. I waved a dismissive hand at her.

"Thanks, Joan. Let's catch up tomorrow. I'll bet Veronica went on up to Max's Aunt Mary's house in Highlands. I want to talk to her too when she comes back." I turned to Bill. "Come on. Let's try those crab cakes. I have a huge need for glass of wine to put this afternoon out of my mind for a little while."

A table for two had been set up by a window facing the swimming pool on the north side of the Inn. Bill pulled the chair out for me and I sat down and took a deep breath. Through the window I could see the twinkling stars. It looked like a normal night in Rosemont—but it certainly didn't feel normal to me.

Felix, the Inn's new waiter, came over and took our drink orders. When he left, I glanced around the dining room. We were alone.

"I remember having spaghetti suppers in this dining room when Joan and I were teenagers," I said. "It was smart of her to turn her childhood home into a bed and breakfast." I paused. "My mother and Joan's mother played bridge in the same bridge club for years. Remember?"

Bill eyes twinkled. "I remember picking you up here when you were supposed to be spending the night with Joan. We had a lot of fun times in our small town." He smiled and then turned serious. "I *don't* remember robberies and murders in the good old days, though."

"Neither do I. But I will never forget the one this afternoon." I shook my head. "I can't imagine that anyone in Rosemont would want to kill Max. No one even knew that he was coming to Rosemont unless Kate told someone. No one on the board even *knew* him. Plus, he was killed in my family's home, a home I want to sell." I looked at Bill again. "We have got to solve this murder soon."

His eyes narrowed. "Look, Simms. There is no 'we.' This could be dangerous. I bet that you are planning to get involved because it is personal for you, but you and Kate and Joan…stay out of it. You can help me the most by telling me about the board members."

I took a sip of my pinot and thought for a minute. How well did I really know the board members? "I think Kate can tell you more. She gave me the skinny on each of them before I joined the board. I can only tell you what I have heard or surmised about them, but I'll try."

I airwrote a list of them, touching each finger as I spoke. "There's Eric Loftis, who is in real estate. He's on the board, I think, for exposure to his business and he wants to sell the McBee Mansion for a nice commission. Then there's Margaret Sellars and Myrtle Meyers—imports from the Junior League. They want to make the fundraiser successful because it would be a feather in their caps. Jackson is only on the board because Kate insisted. They've been a couple for at least a year." I took a sip of my wine. "Maddie Taylor has her fingers in every pie in Rosemont. She has a lot of local connections. And Sally Goldman. She is the owner of Mark and Goldman Ad Agency."

"How about Kate?"

"Oh, Bill, Kate couldn't even kill a gnat on her face, much less Max."

He hesitated. "And you?"

I threw up my hands. "I am not a killer, Bill. I know I am the only one who actually *knew* Max—except, of course, Veronica. We have got to find Veronica, Bill. She may be the clue to this whole tragedy."

"Yes, that is a possibility, but I'm still concerned about the 'we.' What makes *you* want to pursue this? Rosemont has a great police department, and they frown on local citizens interfering."

Tears formed in my eyes and I tried to sniff them away. "Can't you see what is happening to me? I am trying to sell a house and it's not sellable, at least right now. But more importantly, I have lost a friend and I am the one who convinced him to come to Rosemont." I reached in my purse for a tissue.

The dining room door swung open, and Sally and Hershel Goldman came in. Sally had changed clothes since the meeting— for some reason that seemed strange. I'd found the body, but I was still dressed as I'd been for the meeting. I scolded myself—I had to stop my mind from going into accusation mode. But, then, if I were a suspect, so were the other board members.

The couple approached our table and I put on a smile. "Sally, you look refreshed," I said. "It has been a terrible afternoon."

"Yes, I know. I threw my rain-soaked clothes in the laundry. I didn't even feel like cooking. Do you realize how all this will impact our fundraiser?"

The two pulled out chairs and joined us. I wasn't sure how I felt about it but Bill seemed delighted. He summoned Felix and we ordered more drinks.

Sally perused the menu and ordered for both of them. "Any new developments since this afternoon?"

Bill took a sip of his drink. "It is still early times."

I figured that was his standard answer when he didn't want to share. It was time to change the subject. Hershel did it for me.

"Bill and I were reminiscing before about old times. I used to caddy for him on the Rosemont Golf Course when we were sixteen. He never let me play with him—and he certainly didn't give me a tip." Everyone at the table laughed but then an awkward silence set in.

Felix brought our food and we all made noises of how yummy the crab cakes were and sipped our wine, but conversation stopped after that. Felix came by with a dessert menu, but we all declined. I was ready to leave. "Felix, would you put our meals on my room?"

Sally stood up and pushed her chair back. "Bill, did you talk to Veronica before she left for the mountains? Hershel was leaving Publix and saw her driving north on Highway 25." She turned to Hershel. "Didn't you say that?"

Hershel nodded. "I am almost sure it was her. She's in several of the publicity photos on Sally's desk. I thought I recognized her behind the wheel." Bill looked up at him, clearly interested, and he quickly added, "That was before I knew about Mr. Everhart. Sally told me that…ugh…Veronica…wasn't at the theater and you might be looking for her. Then it slipped my mind."

Bill glanced at me and then back at Hershel. "Thanks for the information. It could be helpful."

We watched as Sally and Hershel walked down the hall and out the front door. *Could Sally have changed because she was soaked with blood—and not rain? Were her clothes wet after the murder? Should I mention it to Bill? Was it important? Did Hershel really see Veronica? Were they making all this up to throw us off track?*

I looked up into Bill's sparkling blue eyes. He grinned. "You have something on your mind," he said. "I can still see the sparks firing off in your brain. Want to share?"

We relocated to the sofa in the lobby, and I began to explain the thoughts that had been rushing through my head. I knew I was too tired to make a lot of sense, but it was important for Bill to know that I suspected Sally but didn't have a good reason. Like all the other board members, I assumed she had never met Max and didn't know him. But chill bumps popped up on my arms and that usually meant I was on to something.

"There is *one* thing," I continued. "Max and Veronica were to perform a few scenes from MacBeth for our fundraiser. I remember a night years ago when the play was being performed at a summer stock theater in Connecticut. One of the actors fell from the stage and broke his arm. Max—who was the director—said that it was the Curse. That could be important, Bill. The Rhett Street Players troupe may be plagued by the Curse."

I'm sure Bill's laughter could be heard across the hotel. "Are you talking about that mumbo-jumbo curse that one of the Macbeth witches has cast on members of your group?"

"No! It's *real*. You and I studied it in English Lit. Of course, since you were on the golf team you may have missed it. You always had a match when we were studying important stuff." I paused. "After Shakespeare wrote Macbeth"—I shivered as I said the name—"the play was performed at Hampton Court for James the First. The scene with the witches did not sit well with the people in the audience who actually practiced witchcraft. Shakespeare had brought them into the public eye."

Bill, still struggling not to smile, gestured for me to continue and I did. "The witches put a spell on the play, and it's been cursed ever since. Saying the name Macbeth on stage—except for when it's said in the script—*will* bring bad luck. Actors have died from this curse. In fact, there are numerous incidents of bad things happening during performances of the play." I paused and took a deep breath. "But there *is* an antidote to get rid of the curse."

"Really?" said Bill in mock seriousness. "If we boil the eye of a newt in a cauldron or do a happy dance, we will find the killer?"

I picked up my purse and marched toward the elevator. Bill was acting like it was a joke. It was too late in the evening, and I was too tired for jokes. He called my name and I turned and waited as he caught up with me. "I'm sorry," he said. "I remember some of that tale," he said. "I'll keep what you have told me in mind." He leaned over and gave me a quick peck on the cheek and disappeared through the door.

As I passed the desk on my way to the room, Joan motioned for me to come over. "Couldn't you manage more than a peck on the cheek? I heard that he and Maureen Hightower broke up over six months ago."

I sighed. "Pulleaze, Joan. I need to find a place to live and sell McBee Mansion. I don't have time for a blazing romance."

When I opened the door to my room, the cord on the Roman shades was swinging. It stopped and a certain furball appeared at the foot of the bed. "Maxie, you and I need to find a real home before you destroy this hotel."

I got ready for bed and climbed in, and the little cat curled up next to me. I patted her on the head. "I'll call Eric and get him to show me some condos that will better suit us. After all, tomorrow *is* another day." I pulled the covers up under my chin and stared at the ceiling.

I'd quoted Scarlett O'Hara in an attempt to make myself feel better but it hadn't. That's because "Double, double toil and trouble" was a more fitting mantra. I turned out the light and fell asleep listening to a soft purr wafting through the darkness.

4

Light streamed through my window. I awoke to a stabbing pain in my head and blood dripped down my forehead. I grabbed an object near the top of my head and threw it across the room.

A pitiful mewing emerged from the end of the bed. I squinted at the screen on my iPhone, which I'd laid on the nightstand. It was only 5:30 in the morning. Realizing what must have happened—that Maxie had been kneading my hair in hopes of an early breakfast and I'd thrown her to the foot of my bed—I rescued her and slid back under the cover, clutching her close to my chest. There was, of course, no blood on my forehead.

When my racing heart calmed down, I went back to sleep and woke again at 10 a.m. I lay in the bed, pondering my options for the day. It was time to look for a real home and start settling into my new life in Rosemont. I sat up and reached for my phone—I needed to make some notes about the kind of place I wanted—and *didn't* want—and text them to Eric. It would save us a lot of time. I didn't want to see condos that *Eric* thought I would like—I wanted to see condos that would feel like "home" for Maxie and me.

Just then, the phone played its silly little tune to tell me that someone had sent me a text.

It was from Kate. Meet me at The Kitchen Table on South Street for lunch at high noon. We need to talk about the future of the Rhett Street Players.

What? My job as director could be in jeopardy? I replied with a check mark from my vast array of emojis.

After feeding Maxie, I made myself a quick cup of coffee and jumped in the shower. By 11:45, I was out the door on the way to my car with a few minutes to spare.

The parking lot of The Kitchen Table was almost full when I arrived. I squeezed the Volvo into a corner spot and rushed through the restaurant's door. Enticing aromas emanated from the kitchen. Sunlight from the large windows in the back of the restaurant spilled into a traditional farmhouse style interior,and I felt better. An old worn wooden table stretched across the back wall with metal stools underneath it. The first floor of the restaurant used to be the old Poinsett Mill. It was like Mama's mill village kitchen.

Kate was sitting at the best booth in the house with a glass of chardonnay in front of her. I joined her and quickly ordered the same. "Do you want to split a pizza?" I asked. "I hear the cauliflower gluten-free crust with caramelized onions and roasted sweet potatoes is a healthy choice."

Kate took a large swig of her wine. ""That's okay by me. I don't care what I eat. The Rhett Street Theater is going up in smoke—along with all our plans. What can we do?"

"Find the killer," I said. *Had I really said that out loud?*

Kate was silent for a moment but then her face brightened. "Why not?" she said. "The faster the killer is found, the faster we can get on with our theater plans." We clinked our glasses together.

I leaned back in my seat. "The only problem is that Bill Randolph has already told me to stay out of it. We could end up with daggers in our backs too. The Rosemont police are more than capable of handling this." I leaned forward. "But, it wouldn't hurt to give them a *little* help," I whispered. "After all, I have as much at stake as you do with the theater group—I'm the director of it. And I can't sell McBee Mansion until this murder is solved."

Our pizza arrived and we began to eat. Neither of us really knew what to do next but we had to do something. "What if *we* just questioned the board members and told Bill everything we learned," I said. "That wouldn't be interfering, would it?"

"Listen," said Kate. "That's exactly what I was thinking. I know Bill has already interviewed most of them but they might tell us something they wouldn't tell him." She grabbed her phone and punched in a code. "I need to call a board meeting anyway to get everyone together and plan a memorial service for Mr. Everhart. We can talk to them then."

She sat back, her eyes wide. "Yes! His service can BE the fundraiser for our theater! All of the donations and memorials would go to benefit our group. We can get lots of famous actors and directors in New York to contribute!"

"That is a great idea," I said. "But, first, we need to clear it with Veronica. Do you know if anyone has talked to her? Hershel Goldman told me that he saw her heading to the mountains on Highway 25." I thought for a second.

"I know—I'll call Max's Aunt Mary. You get the board meeting set up."

Kate checked the calendar on her iPhone. "I think we should meet next week. That will give the board members time to change any commitments they have."

I took a sip of my wine and nodded in agreement. "Let's think about what *we* remember about the meeting. I think everyone was sitting at the table before the lights went out. Did you see anyone get up before the room went dark? I didn't. Could the set designers that were building upstairs have anything to do with this? Do you know them well?"

Kate shook her head. "Matt has been a volunteer since we formed this troupe. I know he wouldn't do anything to sabotage our theater. Shelia just started volunteering recently. She isn't from Rosemont but is a great artist and will paint scenery for us. Neither of them knew Max and I don't think they even knew that Max and Veronica were coming."

I knew that Max had a terrible temper—there were lots of theater people that disagreed with his directing methods. What if some crazed and disgruntled actor from New York had done this? No, that was too farfetched. No one would come all the way from New York to kill Max.

I finished my wine and grabbed my purse. Kate and I split the bill and I stood up to leave. As I turned toward the door, Myrtle Meyers and her daughter, Mary Lynn, came charging toward us.

Mary Lynn was unmarried and still living at home. She had made her debut several years ago but had not found her Prince Charming. At least that is what my Aunt Stacy used as the aphorism for "old maid." I plastered a smile on my face. Kate and I said hello and Myrtle put her hand on my shoulder.

"Dear Simmons," she said. "Please don't tell anybody that I hid under the table during that storm. It would make me look like a weakling to my colleagues. I wasn't shirking my duties. I was really afraid. We must all stand together at this horrible time. Come, Mary Lynn. Our table is ready."

I barely held in my laughter until I got out the door. Kate was laughing too. "It really isn't funny, though," I said. "She is from an older generation of Southern women. I think that is exactly what our mothers would have said." Kate agreed.

The Volvo was hot inside, and I let the A/C run for a couple of minutes before I pulled out of the parking lot. While I waited, I checked my messages. Eric wanted me to meet him at River Oaks Condos that afternoon—he had a couple of two- and three-bedroom condos to show me. I texted him back that I would meet him there. That would still give me time to go back to the Inn and check on Maxie.

The parking lot was crowded at the Inn, but I found a space near the driveway and hurried into the much cooler building. Joan called my name as I walked through the door. When I approached the desk, she handed me two messages and then turned to answer the phone. The Inn always seemed to be busy.

When I opened my door, Maxie was curled up in the middle of the bed. Her calico markings stood out in the bright sunshine that came through the window by the bed. I slipped off my shoes, stretched out next to her and read the messages. One was from Max's Aunt Mary—Veronica had not been in Highlands, and she had talked with Detective Randolph. "I'll see you soon," she'd said. Was she coming down to Rosemont?

The other message was from Bill, asking me to call him. I picked up my phone but realized it was almost time to meet Eric. I would have to call Bill later. I put my shoes back on and headed toward the River Oaks Condos.

Eric was waiting on the steps of the condo he'd told me about. As I rushed up the steps, he looked at his watch. "What are we looking at? Is this the three-bedroom condo?" I said as I stepped up beside him.

He glared at me. "Next time you plan to be late, please let me know," he said. He unlocked the realtors' box and opened the door. Immediately, we were met with an old smoke smell and I almost gagged. I backed out the door and tried to stifle my cough. "I can assure you I'm not interested in this one."

Eric shrugged. "I didn't think you would be, but my office has the listing and I thought I'd try it. The other unit is around the corner."

This time, we stepped into a brightly lit hallway. The walls were a creamy white, the perfect background for my extensive art collection. The kitchen was small but well-proportioned—the counter tops were granite and the stove was a great size for a one-person cook. I rubbed my hand across the stainless-steel sink. The place looked well-kept and the asking price was a bargain.

I turned to Eric. "I like this one a lot," I said. "This is a perfect location, but I would like to see a couple more before I make a final decision. Do you have any other listings in this area?"

"Not at the moment. I'll check with the office to see if any new listings have come in and let you know." He paused. "Oh, there's one other thing. Did you get rid of that mangy cat? I didn't see it this morning when I went over to check the house."

"She's at the inn. Eric, I am going to keep the cat. I had Jim Allen check her over and she isn't mangy. She is great company and I have always wanted a cat, but I couldn't have one in New York. My apartment building didn't allow pets."

He shook his head. "Then I'm afraid I have bad news. River Oaks doesn't allow pets either. It is one of their basic rules. To buy here, you will have to get rid of the cat."

I felt tears in my eyes but quickly decided I would not let this upset me. In the middle of all that was going on, I could not deal with getting rid of a cat that I was already becoming attached to. I had moved back to Rosemont to leave old memories behind. Eric would have to find a place that allowed my cat. I changed the subject.

"Kate and I had lunch at the Kitchen Table today. That place has great food. Have you eaten there yet?"

Eric nodded. "Just a couple of days ago, I took a few clients. We liked the place. It's becoming a local hang-out. Myrtle and Mary Lynn were there and I also heard Mayor James eats there every day."

"That's funny," I said. "Myrtle and Mary Lynn were there today, too. I heard that neither of them likes to cook. Myrtle was in a tizzy and as soon as she saw me, she came running over."

"Why?"

"Well, when the lights went out at the board meeting, she rolled herself into a ball and hid under the table—and I almost fell over her. She didn't want me to tell anyone. People would think she was shirking her duty, she said."

"She did not," said Eric, laughing.

"She did too. She rolled out from under the table and scampered up the front stairs."

"Yeah, I saw her go up as I headed to the front door to see if the fuse box was in the shed. That's when I lost my wallet—the one you found when you were trying to get the cat."

I focused on what he had just said. That meant Myrtle couldn't be the killer.

The two of us walked together to the parking lot and I refocused on my mission. "Eric, please find me a great condo on this side of town," I said. "But I want a place that will take pets."

He opened the door to his Audi SUV and was down the driveway before I'd even put on my seat belt. I turned the corner at Pine Street and headed back to the Rosemont Inn.

5

I passed Publix and veered into the parking lot. Maxie needed more cat food and I needed what Aunt Stacy called a "bed-time snack." I loved having popcorn and a glass of wine while I watched Netflix.

I closed the door of the Volvo and headed for the front of the grocery store. Once inside, I glanced around—the aisles were crowded. Everybody who lived on Earl Street was looking for something to cook for dinner. I made a mental note to tell Eric to show me one of the downtown condos.

I pushed the buggy around a corner and bumped into another cart. The woman behind it was familiar. A streak of pink ran down the middle of her black hair and cascaded into a ponytail. Red paint was splattered across the front of her shorts. I fumbled for her name and then it came to me. She was part of the Rhett Street Players and often helped with the set.

"Shelia! Fancy running into you here!"

She smiled. "I live right around the corner."

The day of the murder flashed across my mind. "Weren't you working on the stage for the Macbeth scene when we were having the board meeting?"

She nodded. "Yes, ma'am, I sure was for part of the day. What happened was a real tragedy!" She covered her mouth with her fingers. "Oops. No pun intended."

"Were you there when it happened?"

"No, Matt and I left when we heard the meeting start. We wanted to get out before the storm."

"Did you see anything…anyone?"

Sheila thought for a moment and shook her head. "Nobody from the meeting came up while we were there. I glanced over at the prop table near the stage as we left and I'm pretty sure the dagger was there then."

I could tell she was waiting to see how I would respond. When I didn't, she continued. "Kate texted me a few minutes ago. She says she wants to have a memorial service for Mr. Everhart that's also a fundraiser. Is that true?"

"I hope it is. Kate and I want to have another board meeting next week." We talked for another minute and then said our goodbyes.

The cat food aisle was mostly empty of people. I guessed that none of the downtown condo people had pets. Maybe that wasn't the right place for me after all. I grabbed a couple of cans and then wandered through the snack aisle, thinking all the while about what Sheila had said.

If she and Matt had left when the board meeting was just starting, then Max had still been alive then. Had he gone straight to the third floor without coming down the hall? I scanned the table in my mind. All of the board members had been there when I arrived, which meant that no one on the board could be guilty.

I found an empty check-out line and pulled my wallet out of my pocketbook. The Rosemont Inn was calling my name.

When I opened the front door, Glenn Miller tunes wafted from the dining room. I could not look at the inn as "home," but I realized I *did* feel welcome there. Joan had proclaimed one night a week for seniors to eat and enjoy the Big Band sounds. She served tomato aspic and other foods that the older set enjoyed.

I tiptoed across the lobby from the dining room and was headed toward the steps when I heard my name. It was Joan. She'd come out of another room and was standing at the front desk, waving me over.

"I have carryout from Thai King on South Laurens," she whispered. "Do you want to join me? I thought you would be hungry."

"Why are you whispering?"

Joan looked around and then leaned over the desk. "I don't want my customers to think that I don't eat here all the time."

I grinned. "Of course, I'll join you." I followed Joan into the kitchen alcove. A small round cherry table draped with a crisp linen cloth was set for two with china and sterling.

"This is beautiful," I said and then frowned. "Did we make a date for dinner? I'm sorry if you've been waiting for me—I guess I didn't put it on my calendar."

Joan shook her head. "Listen, dear friend, I *was* waiting, but for Jim. He had a last-minute emergency at the animal clinic, and I don't like to eat by myself." She pulled out one of the chairs and sat down. "Besides, I need food and girl talk. Dating an animal vet is almost as bad as waiting for Godot. Do you remember when we tried to interpret that for our final English exam?"

I sat down opposite Joan and looked around the room, which had once been her family's breakfast nook. The walls were painted a creamy white. Our placemats, from the Kitchen Station, enhanced her Lenox pattern. I slipped a silver ring off a matching linen napkin and placed it in my lap.

The food smelled divine. I hadn't realized how hungry I was. I dipped my spoon into the Tom Kha—the Thai King version was made with coconut milk—and closed my eyes to savor it.

"Oh, yes, I remember *Waiting for Godot*. We had a lot of fun in that AP English class. Then all of our group scattered to different colleges." I thought about all the old friends I'd run into. "I feel like I'm at a reunion since so many of us have moved back to Rosemont."

"Not all of us have really moved back," said Joan. "I mean, you are living in my inn and don't seem to be settled. I certainly don't mind being paid, but you need to find a *real* place to live."

"Eric has shown me several condos but I haven't found anything that feels right. Plus, now that I have adopted a stray cat, I need a bigger place. Any ideas?"

"Well, actually, I have a great idea. And before you say absolutely not, think about all the positives. There are plenty of benefits."

I had a funny feeling. "Benefits to what?"

Joan hesitated. "Moving into McBee Mansion. It would be perfect for you for right now."

I looked at her in disbelief. "Are you crazy? That place is haunted and must cost a fortune to heat—if the furnace even works."

I finished my soup and Joan took our bowls and disappeared into the kitchen. A few seconds later she returned with our entrées—Thai green curry with beef. Thinly sliced beef simmered with eggplant and red pepper. I ate a few bites and set my fork down. "Sumptuous," I exclaimed.

Then I looked at my host with a smirk. "Okay. For a meal this good, I am willing to *listen* to why I should move into the old homeplace."

Joan launched into a litany of reasons—she had obviously thought through what she thought I needed to hear. The place was fully furnished and I wouldn't have to buy furniture. A place looks better to sell if someone lives there because buyers want to picture themselves in the setting of the house.

I had to admit that I could relate to that. So far, I couldn't picture myself in any of the condos Eric had shown me. For someone in such a hurry to sell the mansion he wasn't doing a great job. "Well, you paint a great picture. Let me think about it for a few days. Eric still hasn't brought a contract for me to sign. I *could* live in it for a few months and not feel rushed to buy something right away."

"Want another splash of wine?" Joan asked. "You're not going out again later, are you?"

"Of course," I said. "This is a great *pinot noir*." I looked at the label. It was French, "Domaine de Valmoissine" from Louis Latour. We touched our glasses together. "*À votre santé!*" I said. "To your health!"

Joan sipped from her glass and leaned back. "Simms, I know you too well. You are *really* worried about Max's murder, aren't you?"

I felt tears sprouting in my eyes. "The worst part of this tragedy is the fact that I am the only one that knew Max. I had no reason to kill him. You don't think Bill suspects me, do you?"

"Don't be absurd. He doesn't think that. And I know he is happy that you are back—he's been showing up in town with a different woman every week. I think the two of you could enjoy more of each other's company. You might find that you have a lot in common."

I ignored what she said, at least for the moment. "Since I didn't kill Max, who do you think did? Kate wants it to be a crazed actor from New York."

"Why would it be?"

"Max had a terrible temper. He fired one of the actors in his last production because she was never on time and always disagreed with him. And, although he was never abrasive with me, I think there were other incidents through his career."

Joan set her glass on the table. "I know it wasn't you or Kate. I'm sure Bill Randolph feels that way too. It *is* his job to find the killer and bring peace to the Rhett Street Players." She thought for a moment. "Veronica is starting to look suspicious. What has happened to her? Would she have a reason to kill Mr. Everhart?"

"They always seemed fine to me. And I have a feeling that Veronica's dead too."

Joan poured herself more wine. "Rosemont is a small place. The killer will probably make a mistake. I know you and Kate want to find out 'who done it' right now. The Rhett Street theater group needs money to operate but it is not worth risking your life. You and Kate need to work on another fundraiser and leave the police work to Bill."

She rolled her eyes. "I know you two. I am sure that you are already snooping around." She lifted the wine bottle. "Have the last splash before you head off to your new kitty and dreamland. And don't think I didn't see the way that Bill looked at you last night—and you at him. You had a fun time at dinner with him. Don't deny it."

I took the final sip of my wine and gave Joan a hug. "I can't believe how much fun it was to relive old times."

"New times are fun too. Remember that when Bill calls."

I blew a kiss to Joan and headed up the steps, memories of a lifetime flooding my mind with every step.

Mother and Daddy had gone to a conference on Sea Island, Georgia, and after much pleading and promises to obey Joan's curfew, I was allowed to stay in Rosemont. I came down these very steps dressed in a sexy black spaghetti-strap sundress and Bill Randolph was waiting at the bottom in his favorite faded blue denim shirt tucked into a pair of dark-washed jeans.

As I turned to go to my room, it hit me that Bill had given me that shirt when I went to New York. He'd been on his way to law school at Virginia and we'd promised to stay together forever. And then, I'd met Michael.

I reached my door and turned the big brass key. I scooped Maxie out of her bed and placed her gently on my pillow. After dropping some kibbles into her bowl, I sat down on the bed.

I knew I would have trouble falling asleep and I did. Too much had happened in the past two days. I grabbed my phone and texted Eric to meet me at the mansion at 10 a.m. His reply was swift. Will bring contract to sell McBee. He must be a night owl, I thought. I glanced at my earlier messages. It was now too late to return Bill's call. Tomorrow and tomorrow and tomorrow.

I stroked Maxie. "Ordinary people have songs on a loop in their minds. Me, I have quotes." She licked my hand. "The thought of tomorrow is right, though," I said. "I need to let go of Michael and the past. I will send the boxes in storage to his parents. I don't need stuff to keep his memory alive. I have his memory in my heart."

I touched my nose to Maxie's and closed my eyes.

6

Sunlight spilled through the window. I glanced at the clock. I had slept all night without waking.

I had just over an hour to meet Eric. After a quick shower, I threw on my new Binova Dress by Conditions Apply. I had hit the sale rack at The Boutique on Augusta when I first got to town. I quickly applied lipstick, grabbed my purse, and walked down the stairs at the Inn. I could smell heavenly aromas coming from the Inn's kitchen. I popped into the dining room and found Bill Randolph tackling a huge plate of blueberry pancakes. He looked up and grinned.

"I decided to eat breakfast while I waited for you to wake up."

I just smiled in response and he continued. "Good night? Joan told me that you all stayed up late and enjoyed a few laughs. I came over because I want to ask you a couple of questions, but I would rather have breakfast with you than talk on the phone."

Just then, Joan arrived at the table. "My usual," I said. Since I had been at the Inn, my order had been the same—coffee, Greek yogurt and fruit. She winked at me and brought my order out right away.

I turned back to Bill. "What is going on with the case? Have you made any progress? Did Veronica go to Highlands? I hope she comes back today. I want to talk to her." I scooped up a spoonful of yogurt as I spoke.

"I want to talk to her too. It appears that she never made it to Rosemont."

"What do you mean?"

"She never left New York. Max got a refund on her plane ticket and came alone."

"She must have snagged a great part and had to go into rehearsals. I heard that there was going to be a revival of Forty-Second Street. The part of Dorothy Brock would be perfect for Veronica."

"Do you know that for sure? I need to make sure that she didn't sneak into Rosemont some other way and then leave. Is there someone in New York that I could contact to find out?"

"Let me think about it. I still think she's key to solving Max's murder, but I truly don't think she would kill Max. I mean, there were always rumors that Max was playing around, but I think it was just the rumor mill spiked by jealousy." I thought for a moment. "I know—I'll get in touch with her agent and let you know."

Bill nodded and I kept talking. "Have you finished with McBee mansion? I am meeting Eric over there this morning. I know he really wants to officially put it on the market. Meanwhile, Joan wants me to move *into* the mansion. My cat and I can't stay here. We need to spread out. It is not fun to step into a litterbox in the middle of the night."

Bill burst out laughing. "Under those circumstances, I think you should move in today. We have cleaned the place and won't need to go back. Let me know when you move." He signed the check and waved as he walked out the door.

I took another sip of coffee and glanced at my iPhone. I had a few minutes before I left for McBee. I glanced through my contacts and found my old work number in New York. Julie, my replacement, picked up on the second ring.

"Forty-Second-Street Theater." There was a pause, during which she must've looked at Caller ID. "Simmons, how are you? Ready to come back to your life in the real world? We miss you."

"Well, I am settling into what you would call a rural existence. I don't hear sirens all night and the air in Rosemont is clean and clear." I hesitated before going on. I knew Julie loved gossip. "I know that you have heard about Max. I found him. The police are trying to get in touch with Veronica. It seems that she didn't come to Rosemont, but no one knows where she is. Any ideas? Should the police try to get in touch with her agent?"

"Well," Julie said, "I have heard the story from three different sources. Max wanted to retire and move to Highlands near his aunt. Veronica's career was taking off. She refused to go and went to Portugal instead. She's filming a movie with Sean Baker. It seems that they are having an affair."

I smiled to myself. "Thought you would know what was going on. I will pass this on to the police. Come see us and meet the Rhett Street Players. You would like Rosemont."

"What I want to know is the secret you wouldn't share with me before you left. Can you tell me now? Wait, ticket sales phone is ringing off the hook. I'll call you back." The call disconnected. I pushed the end button on my phone and ate the last bite of my yogurt.

I walked out of the Inn in already hot air. Even warmer air blew in my face when I opened the driver's door to the Volvo, so I let down my window and quickly turned on the air conditioner. I punched the number on Bill's card into my phone and left the message about Veronica. I could mark her off of my list of suspects.

Hearing Julie's voice made me think of how much I loved the theater and my secret desire to write a play that a troupe like the Rhett Street Players could perform. I would remind Kate that I wanted to do that. I wouldn't let Max's murder or anything else stop me.

Eric stood on the porch of McBee Mansion as I drove up. He tapped his watch as I walked up the steps. His blue eyes were sparkling. I was definitely attracted to him.

"You have a nasty habit of being late," he said. "My daddy told me that time is money." He turned toward the front door. "Let's get started. I have a few things to show you. I don't think this place will pass inspection unless you fix them. But as I said at the meeting, I may be able to sell the property to a developer that will tear down the mansion and build condos on this site."

"You would do that? This is a downtown historic district. I don't think the City Council will go for that."

"I have Frank Myers in my back pocket and his wife is on the board. Just watch me." He turned toward the door. "Come on. I have a showing over on the east side in 30 minutes. I want you to see the water marks in the downstairs study. It may take a bit to get that fixed. Margaret Sellers told me the other day at the board meeting that this old mansion was a piece of junk and her husband Joe would love to see an improvement."

I shuddered. I don't think Margaret meant tear it down. I followed Eric into the study. He walked over to the closet and opened the door. I could see water marks running down the back wall—it was still wet. I reached in to touch it and the back wall fell over. "Now, look what you've done," said Eric. "That is going to cost even more. I'll get a carpenter to come and give us an estimate. We can save money by putting plywood on that wall. No one will know the difference."

I would know the difference, I thought. I looked in again and stopped short. Behind the wall was another door! I turned the knob and the door opened. A musty dank smell permeated the small space. "I'm going to the kitchen to get a flashlight," I said. "Uncle Hugh and Daddy never mentioned a secret passage."

"Please wait until I have time to explore with you," Eric said. "There are probably rats and spiders and all kinds of bugs in that space. I have to go if I am going to meet my client now. Let's meet tomorrow and I won't book any other showings. Don't go in there alone. There could be snakes too."

"You're right," I said. "The floor could fall in and I could break my leg. Or get snake bitten."

I waved to Eric as he went out the door and waited until I heard his car start before I headed straight to the kitchen for a flashlight. Ducking through the closet, I took a tentative glance into a dark cave and slowly walked down dirt steps to a dirt floor in the basement. This was obviously a tunnel. First it went toward the front of the house but then turned toward the back. It was longer than I expected, but there were no snakes, bugs or scary shadows. It was clear that the tunnel had not been used for a long time.

Then, I saw a faint sliver of light ahead. Wow, I thought. A light at the end of a tunnel! What a good feeling! I turned off the flash-light and was climbing up a bank toward an opening when I felt a small hole in the wall. I stuck my hand in and felt a rusty old tin. I dusted it off and after a couple of tries pried it open. I turned the flashlight back on and pointed it at the tin. Inside were old pieces of paper with what looked like hand-drawn maps to somewhere else.

I closed the tin and put it back in the wall. It was then that I noticed that just beyond the indentation was something that might once have been an entrance to a small room. I would definitely have to have that investigated. I crawled up the bank toward the light and squeezed through and out. I knew immediately where I was—a few blocks from the mansion closer to downtown on the Reedy River.

I needed to do some googling and take a trip to the South Carolina Room at the library. Great Aunt Addie Black had shared secret stories about the mansion. Maybe Aunt Stacy would remember stories she had heard, but I wouldn't tell her yet. I had to keep this to myself until I was sure.

I could picture my great-granddaddy making "bathtub gin" and sending it north on the river toward larger cities. Or maybe even running a speakeasy during the 1920s. But the tunnel had to be older than that, from a much earlier time. Could McBee Mansion have been a stop on the Underground Railroad?

If that were true, the house could be saved from developers. Developers wouldn't be able to tear down a historic site. The thrill of the idea made me realize that I loved the mansion—and the history that made it part of a much bigger picture.

I felt sweat run down my back and wiped my forehead—I was beyond the "glistening" stage! I staggered the two blocks back to the mansion above ground. I walked into the kitchen to put the flashlight away and then opened the refrigerator. A pitcher of tea was left over from the board meeting. I gulped down a couple of glasses and wandered through the mansion with new eyes. Joan was right. Maybe it *was* livable! The fireplace in the study had a marble surround. I could see myself by the fire with a hot buttered rum and Maxie on my lap.

Newly energized, I started from the back and counted the rooms—there were 22—and all of them needed work. It wasn't falling apart around my ears, but the kitchen needed more work than a mining camp kitchen. Was I willing to take on this project?

It seemed doable. I thought of the beautiful fireplaces and the gorgeous views of the upstate mountains. And, like Joan said, I could make it my temporary home and could move in until Eric sold it. There would be plenty of time to find the right condo.

A jarring ring interrupted my thoughts. Where was my phone? I followed the sound to the mantle in the study. It was Kate.

"You aren't going to believe this," she said. "Veronica has run off with another man. Max's Aunt Mary told me. She never came to Rosemont. Bill Randolph says the police have narrowed their suspects." She paused. "On another note, I have confirmation from all the board members that we can get together next week and plan a memorial service for Max. I think his Aunt Mary wants to come to the meeting. Do you think Eric will let us use McBee while he's trying to sell it? He told me he had a prospect coming from Connecticut next week."

My mind was racing. "He didn't tell me that. He was too busy today to even go through the house with me. And yes, I heard about Veronica. That is really sad." Kate said nothing, so I took a breath and continued. "Whether we can have the meeting isn't Eric's decision anyway. I have some other news you haven't heard. I am moving into McBee until I find the condo I want. I will lose my mind if I have to stay at the Inn for the rest of the summer."

"What will Joan think?"

"Actually, it was her idea. The room I have isn't big enough for me and Maxie to be comfortable for a long time. My plan right now is to restore the study and write a play. We'll get the Rhett Street Players to perform it and raise more money. What do you think?"

Kate squealed. "I think that is the best news ever. When do you plan to move? I will help you."

"I have just decided that I want to move in by Saturday. I have four suitcases and six boxes. My condo in New York was furnished and the Pettigrus took most of the furniture from the house in Connecticut. It won't take me long."

We made plans to get together the next day and Kate said goodbye. For the first time since I had returned to Rosemont, I felt like I belonged there.

7

The Rosemont Library was almost empty, but when I dropped the book on the table with a thud, the three people who were there looked up from their reading and glared at me.

Aunt Stacy and I had looked through every book we could find about Rosemont during the Civil War. We had been researching for a week and needed to compare notes. I crept over to where my aunt was sitting and whispered to her. "Let's go across the street to Cookies and Cream. We can talk and figure out what to do." She closed the book she was reading and followed me as I led the way across the street.

I ordered my usual latte—despite the heat, I'd had one twice a day for the last month I lived in New York. Aunt Stacy got a glass of iced tea, and we started comparing notes. She had found that the Reedy ran into the Saluda River and traced the flow of the water to the coast.

"Wasn't that one way to freedom for some? I asked.

"I need to talk to Carol Chambers," she said. "She is President of the Rosemont Historical Society this year. She can tell us more about Rosemont in the mid-1800s, but I *did* read one interesting article in a book about signals of the Underground Railroad. The houses providing refuge often displayed quilts that let people know it was a safe house. A framed quilt hangs over the fireplace in the McBee downstairs study. Do you know what I mean?"

"Yes. The quilt that your great-grandmother Minnie sewed. That would have been in the 1800s." A chill ran up my spine. "Aunt Stacy, I think you are on to something. The quilt in the study is called Evening Star. Quilts *were* used as secret codes. I just read that while you were looking up the newspaper clippings in that era."

"Wait until Carol hears this!" Aunt Stacy grabbed her bag and blew me a kiss. "I have errands to run. See you later." She almost ran over Maddie Taylor as she hurried out the door.

Maddie looked at her and then at me. "I haven't seen your Aunt Stacy move that fast in a long time. What's she up to these days?" Maddie Taylor asked.

"She's helping me with the history of the McBee Mansion. We want to get it on the Historic Register. It would be a great benefit to the Historical Society if we did."

Maddie put her pile of gardening books on the table and got a latte for herself from the counter. Like Myrtle, she was one not to hold back her opinions at meetings.

I knew that she was younger than Myrtle, but they had been friends for a long time. Natives of Rosemont stuck together and were either lifetime friends or sworn enemies, but either way, they clung together like memories in a scrapbook. Yes, even if they were enemies.

I had heard that the last time Maddie's husband won the pot at the club poker night, Myrtle Myers's husband called Mr. Taylor a cheater and vowed never to play with him again. But it had obviously not affected Maddie and Myrtle's friendship.

Maddie took a sip of her coffee. "I guess you have heard the latest news about the murder. It's a shame that Veronica couldn't have done it. Jackson told me that he and Kate think a crazed actor from New York followed Max here and stabbed him. It makes sense. None of us had opportunity or motive. Would you know anything about an actor that had a vendetta?"

I shrugged my shoulders. "When Max agreed to come to Rosemont, he was donating his time and expertise to help our theater. Kate will address this at our meeting. She has a few ideas for raising money. Fingers crossed." I said.

I thought it was a good idea to change the subject. "What do you know about Jackson? Have he and Kate been seeing each other for a long time? She mentioned him in several emails and texts before I came here. He's an investment banker? I know he isn't from Rosemont. She seems happy, doesn't she?"

Maddie nodded. "She's happier than she has ever been. About Jackson—I know that he came to Longstreet Investments from Chicago. At the time I thought he was crazy to leave a large firm and move here. My husband did some checking and it seems that he didn't make as many profitable investments as the company wanted. The investment business in Chicago is cutthroat. In Rosemont, it is more laid back and Jackson has adapted."

She suddenly stood up. "I must be going," she said. "I will see you at the meeting. I have to decide what to plant in my back garden. I will win the blue ribbon for my camellias, but I am going to enter an arrangement in the cut flower category." Maddie grabbed her planting guidebooks and pulled the door to the coffee shop open. A blast of hot air penetrated the shop.

I realized I was hungry and wanted one of Aunt Stacy's summer tomato sandwiches. My mind drifted. This time next year, I would have a garden in my back yard. I would join the Mary Alice Gibson Garden Club and become part of the community. But for now, I could ride out to the Tomato Basket, I thought. Their tomatoes were to die for.

I stopped myself. "To die for" brought horrible images into my mind. I shook my head and took a deep breath.

As I drove down Parker Avenue, I swore to myself that I would not let anyone stop me from writing my play. The Rhett Street Players would be my first off-off-off Broadway production. Early afternoon was usually slow at the Inn, so I headed back to the Inn to get Joan to ride with me if she could take the time.

It had become a habit for me to pull the Volvo into the corner space of the Inn's parking lot, but it was a habit that would be easy to break—I was getting excited about moving to McBee. I had postponed it for a week in my mind, but I had already packed most of my things and would move by the end of the week.

Joan was grabbing her straw tote as I approached the desk. "I was about to call you," she said. "You and Bill, Kate and Jackson, and Jim and I are going to Farris Hill tomorrow for a real summer picnic."

I made a face. "I'm not sure that's a good idea. Bill is investigating a murder that involves me. Every time we've been together, he's questioned me about something. I'll pass."

"Come on. He's the one who suggested the picnic. We are going to the Tomato Vine to get new potatoes, tomatoes and anything else we can eat at a picnic. We can also get cans of white wine to put on ice. You do have a decent bathing suit, don't you? I bet that you never went swimming in New York."

Thoughts of Michael swimming laps at the Fifth Avenue Club popped into my mind. I always sat on the side of the pool and watched. Maybe I could think of an excuse to watch—I had always hated getting my face wet because when I was nine, my cousin Ted held my head underwater to see if I could hold my breath longer than his sister Liz. He still thinks that was funny.

"I'll see what I can find," I said. "Since I am moving on Friday, I really don't want to unpack boxes and suitcases, but I could be the lifeguard."

The Tomato Basket parking lot was full, so we parked across the street and jaywalked over to the entrance. The open-air building was anchored with a concrete floor. Baskets of fresh produce spilled onto the counters. Vendors from all over the area filled their stands with home grown produce. There were peanuts and corn for popping and every vegetable imaginable. I took a deep breath—I could smell ripe onions, garlic and fresh tomatoes for a marinara sauce. As soon as I moved into McBee, I would make Anthony's sauce. He lived around the corner from my apartment in New York and had often shared some of his mother's Italian cooking with me.

The aroma of fresh baked bread lured me down the center aisle. but I stopped when I heard a commotion at the other end. Myrtle Myers was clinging to a basket of peaches as if the basket were made of gold. Her daughter, Mary Lynn, was trying to jerk it away. "We aren't going to make peach preserves this year. We still have jars of the stuff in our pantry. Be reasonable."

Myrtle yanked the basket away and swung it around. More than a dozen peaches fell out of the basket and rolled across the floor. "See what you did," Myrtle screamed. "I can't even trust you to go shopping with me!" She threw her hand out and swiped all the baskets off the stand. Then she proceeded to stomp the peaches as if they were grapes in a vat.

A crowd had started gathering and I spotted Joan coming my way. Kate, who she'd found somewhere else in the store, was following on her heels. They arrived just in time to hear Mary Lynn shout at her mother. "If you say one more mean word to me, I will tell the Rhett Street actors what really happened. And don't think I won't." Mary Lynn picked up a peach and threw it across the aisle. She stormed through the crowd and ran to her mother's car.

Mrs. Jones, whose peaches had been squashed, wrote up a ticket for the entire lot and handed it to Myrtle. "You can pay at the register on your way out. Thank you for buying all my peaches. I needed to go home early."

"Well, I never," said Myrtle, as she snatched the ticket and turned to walk toward the door. Kate, Joan, and I blocked her way, and I grabbed her arm and marched her to the register while Kate and Joan tried to avoid stepping on the peaches. Juice on the concrete floor from the ones Myrtle had smashed had already attracted flies and bees from the woods behind the store.

A woman screamed and dropped a cotton bag full of tomatoes. "I have been stung by a huge flying insect," she said. The man behind her stepped on one of the tomatoes, slipped and caught her by the bottom of her dress. They both landed in front of a display of sliced watermelon.

The woman turned to slap the man and instead hit a watermelon and the display came rolling down. Juice from the quarter-cut melons mixed with the peaches and trickled toward the cash register. A little boy looked down and squinched his face.

"Mommy, I think I'm going to throw up," he said.

I snatched Myrtle's hand. "Let's get out of here before they sue all of us. You have bought all the peaches in the store, so it's time to go." Kate and Joan quickly followed us and we regrouped in the parking lot. Mary Lynn had started the car and the air was cool and quiet. I almost shoved Myrtle inside.

Kate stuck her head inside the car. "Confess right now or I will call Bill Randolph. What don't you want us to know about Max's death? Did you kill him?"

Myrtle blew her nose and wiped the tears from her face. "I am afraid of storms and hid under the table. After the storm passed, I crawled out and went to the stairs. The lights came on and Eric saw me. I told him that I had been looking for the fuse box. He told me to come back into the dining room and then I heard Simmons scream. Mary Lynn thinks I have a weak backbone and threatens to tell my friends that I won't watch scary movies or stay by myself at night. I am really afraid of thunder and lightning. Please don't tell anyone."

Kate shook her head. "You should tell a psychologist," she whispered, but Myrtle didn't hear her—Mary Lynn had already put the car in reverse and was moving quickly toward the exit.

We all turned and walked back to Joan's car. I turned to Kate. "I told Joan that I would meet to help with the picnic but I am *not* going back in there. I suggest that we pick up food from the Chef's

Cottage on the way to Farris Hill. We can get the guys to help us pick out the food." I wanted nothing more than to get back to the Inn and wash off my shoes. Then Maxie and I could have some play time. It had been a long day.

8

It was a glorious day for a picnic, but the picnic turned into a cookout. Once the guys got involved, we had to pack a grill, burgers, slaw and chips. Joan and Jim rode with Bill and me. Kate and Jackson were in a truck behind us with all the supplies and the grill.

I was certain all of this was specifically for me to have time with Bill Randolph, but I didn't know if he was aware of what Joan and Jim were up to at this point. I wanted to ask him about the progress on Max's murder but I kept my mouth shut. Maybe he would volunteer information before the day was over. I looked over at his curly brown hair and smiled. He gave me a half-smile and kept his eyes on the road.

We headed up to Farris Hill—less than a mountain but more than a hill. I remembered getting my YMCA swimming certificate on Farris Lake. The park was formerly part of a country club that had been abandoned years before. Now it was a local hangout for Rosemonters and was only a few miles from downtown.

We turned off the Buncombe Road and headed up Highway 25. I glanced at Bill. "I guess Veronica didn't come up Highway 25 after all. Hershel must have been mistaken. Maybe Hershel did it!

Something's fishy, don't you think?"

"Hmmm." This was the only response I heard from Bill. Obviously, he wasn't willing to volunteer any information about the case with me.

Joan must have been listening in because she leaned over the front seat. "Have you found anything that is getting you closer to solving the case?"

Bill again revealed nothing, so we all grew silent and watched the scenery go by. We passed a farm stand and pulled into the park. Jackson and Kate pulled in beside us.

It was almost high noon. While the guys unloaded Jackson's truck, I helped Joan and Kate put a plastic cloth over a picnic table. Jackson started the grill and Kate threw some peaches beside the burgers. I knew she had not gone back to the Tomato Basket. "Are the peaches fresh?" I asked.

"Fresh from the gas station stand on Augusta Road. I do not plan to go back to the Basket anytime soon."

Bill lifted his head. "What happened at that crazy open-air stand? A report came across my desk yesterday that some deranged person started a fight and the owner called the police."

It took a while but Joan and Kate recounted the fight beween Myrtle and her daughter, with all the gory details. Lunch was ready by the time they finished, and we sat down at the table. The peaches looked grilled to perfection, and I piled more slaw on my burger. Jackson and Jim were laughing but Bill looked sober. "Tell me again about Myrtle and what she said."

I bit into my burger and listened to Kate tell the story. "What does that have to do with the murder?" I asked.

"Probably nothing. I think that there is anger—a lot of issues in the Meyers family."

I was sure that wasn't really what he was thinking, but I still couldn't believe that Myrtle would stab Max. But could her daughter Mary Lynn? No, that was absurd. I bet Mary Lynn had no idea what was going on at the theater.

I stretched and yawned. "Let's take a walk around the lake—I think it's about a mile. A chorus of no's assaulted me. Jackson and Kate spread a blanket on the ground. Joan and Jim had already headed out to climb Farris Hill.

Bill grabbed my hand. "I'll walk with you." He held my hand and we walked to the edge of the lake. It gave me a comfortable feeling. I looked over and smiled and he smiled back. "I'm glad that the three of you aren't getting into my investigation," he said.

I figured this wasn't the time to confess that I was determined to make sure that Max's killer was caught and justice served. There were lots of suspects and not many clues. The New York police would be looking for an actor with a grudge. It was as plausible as any other theory.

Halfway around the lake I stopped. The banks were lush with mountain laurel. I hopped up on an outcropping of rocks, and Bill sat down beside me. I looked across the lake and something seemed odd. Instead of seeing green trees and blooming wildflowers, I saw a tree limb a few feet into the water. I punched Bill and pointed at the branch. Bill jumped up. "That's not a limb. That's an arm."

I screamed and Bill dove into the lake. After splashing around, he swam out to the body and pulled it to shore. I met him on the other side.

The body was instantly identifiable. It was Veronica. There was no light in her eyes. Her body was stiff. "Call 911," Bill gasped. I reached into my pocket and punched the numbers into my iPhone.

Jackson and Kate came running. "Your voice echoed across the lake," Kate said. "We thought you had been attacked by a bear." She looked down at the body, and then immediately turned around and threw up. Joan and Jim trotted up to the rocks. Joan started crying and Jim held her tightly and led her away.

Sirens blared in the distance. Although it was hot outside, Bill's teeth were chattering. "I'll go get a blanket," I said. Bill leaned over the body and nodded.

A million thoughts raced through my mind. Did Hershel Goldman follow Veronica up to the park? Did my friend in New York lie to me about Veronica getting a part in Sean's movie? Did the same person kill Veronica and Max? I grabbed the blanket from the ground and headed back to Bill.

"We're leaving," shouted Kate from the picnic table. "Get a ride home with Bill."

When the official vehicles arrived, I sat on a bench by the picnic table. Two hours passed before the scene had been cleared and Bill trudged up the hill to the table. His curly hair was plastered to his head and his damp clothes clung to his body. I reached out to him but he looked up when a voice behind me called his name.

"Bill, are you okay? I was on my way to your house and found out that you were up here. Are you okay?"

A tall thin woman who looked like she had just stepped off the cover of *Vogue* ran up and hugged him. He smiled and hugged her back and then turned to me. "I'll get you a ride with Sgt. Hawkins."

I was sitting in the patrol car with the police officer before I really knew what had happened. I watched Bill and his girlfriend—or even significant other—walk back to his car. I sighed and tried not to think about Veronica.

The officer turned to look at me. "Really terrible. We haven't had a double murder here in years—maybe never. I reckon Detective Randolph has his work cut out for him."

"Do you think he has a handle on what has happened?" I asked. If Bill wouldn't tell me anything then maybe Hawkins would be more forthcoming.

"He sure spent a lot of time interrogating that yardman that takes care of McBee Mansion. The man must have seen something suspicious. I haven't had a chance to read his report, but I bet Detective Randolph will solve this soon. It has really kept out department busy."

I tried not to look too interested, but I wanted him to keep talking. There was no way that the McBee estate would have been paying for a yardman. Could it have been a homeless person? Or maybe this person was planning to rob the mansion and didn't realize that there would be people around that afternoon. I had a lot to think about. We drove the rest of the way in silence.

Kate and Joan were waiting for me on the steps of the Inn. We all charged into the breakfast nook and I joined them for a glass of pinot noir. "Do either of you know who the yardman is for McBee?" I said. "I didn't know we had one. I thought volunteers were going to clean up the grounds before the fundraiser."

"Why do you ask?" said Kate.

"Hawkins said that the police had questioned a yardman."

Kate shook her head. "We haven't hired anyone. We need to find out who this person is and why Bill suspects him. Maybe Eric knows something. I'll ask him—I have to call him about the agenda for our board meeting anyway."

"I think I should join the board," said Joan. "If we are going to work on this, we should all be on the same page."

Kate and I both shouted a rowdy yes and we all clinked glasses. I suddenly didn't feel so alone.

"Why didn't Bill bring you back? Did he have to go straight to the station?"

I shrugged. "I got pawned off on his sergeant when his girlfriend showed up."

"You mean Lucy?" Joan said. "She came by here looking for him. We told her what had happened."

"You told her where to find him and knew I was with him? You really *are* good friends," I said sarcastically.

Joan and Kate burst into laughter. "Was this woman tall and slender and look like a model?" asked Joan. When I nodded, she continued. "That's because she *is* a model for the Ford agency in New York. She doesn't get home often."

"How long have they been together?" I asked.

Kate looked at me like I'd lost my mind. "Most of their lives," she said. "She's Bill's younger sister. You remember her. She would follow us and beg to play when we were playing Red Rover at dusk in your backyard."

My jaw dropped. "Not the scrawny, tangle-haired, pigeon-toed kid that we laughed at!" I leaned back in my chair. "Boy, she turned into a swan, didn't she?"

I hoped that Joan and Kate hadn't seen the relief in my face. It was still too soon for me to kindle a fire with Bill but the embers were definitely sparking.

"I think I will take popcorn and wine up to my room," I said. "I need to check on Maxie. She has been alone all day. My meager belongings are ready to throw in the Volvo in the morning after breakfast—I hope she will like her new home."

After hugs and promises that we would find the elusive "yardman" and maybe have the murders cleared up soon, I left Kate and Joan sharing the rest of the bottle of red wine and carried a small wicker basket with food up the stairs.

As soon as I opened the door, I heard Maxie meow. I scooped her up and we sat on the bed. I shared bites of my chicken sandwich with her and she curled up in my lap and purred. I peered out the window and thought I saw a shadow moving near my car. Could that be the yardman that I didn't know we had?

I squinted my eyes and realized that it was only a tree branch waving in front of the streetlamp. I put Maxie on my pillow and closed the shades. I had trouble going to sleep for a while—I kept seeing Veronica's arm in the lake—but finally, I fell into a deep sleep on top of the bed.

9

Aunt Stacy was standing on the porch when I pulled up in front of McBee with all my worldly possessions. She wanted a tour of the tunnel. I'd have to wait until later to settle in.

Within minutes, we stood at the entrance inside, our flashlights at the ready. It took me a few tries to get the false door open. I pointed my flashlight into the darkness. "Would you like to go first?"

"You have already explored some," said Aunt Stacy. "I'll follow you."

I stepped into nothingness, which was darker than the back side of the moon. The weak beam of my flashlight barely made a dent. I felt Aunt Stacy's hand on my shoulder. "Let's look for clues that this was part of the Underground Railroad," she said.

We edged our way down the middle of the tunnel. It was a narrow path but large enough for a single person to walk through. I felt the cold hard dirt press against my hand. It took a long time to go a short distance. Aunt Stacy tried to get me to flash the beam in different directions.

"Have you finished your research at the library?" I said. "Maybe some tunnels had descriptions or directions of how to build them."

Aunt Stacy shrugged. "You just dig a tunnel and hang out your quilt. The key will be to have the framed quilt that is hanging over the mantle authenticated. The Rosemont Historical Society will help us with that."

"This is *your* project," I replied. "I need to get McBee Mansion in a semblance of order. We need to put this place on the market as soon as possible. We want top dollar for it."

"How could you even think that the family could let go of this magnificent place? We have owned this land for generations. We can't throw it away for some cheaply built stack of high-rise condos. I absolutely forbid you to do that."

I couldn't see Aunt Stacy's face in the darkness, but I could feel the hurt in her words. I had never discussed selling the house with her. The place had been left to me and none of the other family members had protested. Now that McBee Mansion might become a historical site, Aunt Stacy was determined to keep it and not sell.

I let the moment pass. Deep in a dark tunnel wasn't the time to discuss important issues. We'd moved along for a few more steps when she stopped. "Let's turn back," she said. "Something is making me sneeze. There is a smell in here that is overwhelming. It is musty—but it's almost like somebody with too much cologne has been here too."

I sniffed the air and understood what she meant. "That's weird," I said. "That cologne smell wasn't here when I came down in the tunnel before."

Aunt Stacy sneezed and her hand pushed my shoulder. I lost my footing, dropped to my knees, and put my hand down to catch myself on the hard dirt surface. I closed my fingers around something slick and screamed. Aunt Stacy pulled me up and started heading back the way that we had come. "It might be a snake," she said.

"Wait," I said, and she beamed her light toward my hand. I was clutching a slim black Montblanc pen. "This belongs to a *human* snake," I said. "Someone else has definitely been in here."

"I knew it! A member of the Historical Society has been spying on me. You know that none of them want us to be on the Historical Register. Not with something like this. Our family was supposed to be loyal supporters of the Lost Cause."

"You are being absurd! No one even knows that we have a tunnel in the house! I think someone was trying to break in to steal some of the valuables. I will pass the pen on to Bill Randolph."

"That's not a good idea either. His great-great grandfather fought alongside General Pettigru in that horrid war and Bill will want to protect his family's name. Don't show it to him."

"Aunt Stacy, that horrid war, as you call it, was more than a hundred and fifty years ago. Bill Randolph probably never even thought about Rosemont's participation in the war. And I promise this will not hurt your chances of getting McBee Mansion on the Registry."

We emerged into the study and I sat down in the desk chair behind Uncle Hugh's massive mahogany desk. Aunt Stacy gathered her purse and jacket. "I'll check with you tomorrow. Please be careful about how you tell Bill where we found the pen."

The door slammed and I sat back and looked at my view of the garden. This would be the perfect spot for inspiration. My play could come to life in this room. This chair was definitely a keeper. I grabbed my iPhone and punched in Bill's number. I left a message and decided to celebrate by cooking Anthony's Italian supper. Maybe I would invite Bill and show him the tunnel. I wanted a focus for our meeting, even if the plan didn't succeed. After making an extensive list, I decided that the Fresh Market would be the best place to grocery shop. I threw my cotton tote bags in the front and walked around the car. That's when I noticed my front tire was flat.

On closer inspection, I realized that the tire had been slashed. So had the left back tire. Chills ran down my back. This wasn't a bad neighborhood. It had to be someone who wanted me to move. I dialed 911.

I was standing in front of my Volvo when the squad car pulled up to the curb. It had taken them a long time to arrive.

Officer Johnson got out of his car and took notes. I was blabbering and couldn't stop. "Someone wants to get even with me," I screamed. I had learned to project while working in the theater, so I could be heard a block away. Neighbors were coming out and several kids on bikes stopped to look at the scene. "Those were new tires. I bought them before I left New York. I want to know who is trying to scare me."

"It probably wasn't a scare tactic," Officer Johnson said. "We have had reports of stolen bikes and other forms of maliciousness this summer. Some of the kids in this area may have been bored and are just pulling pranks on the neighbors."

"This was no prank." I had calmed down enough to quit yelling. "I intend to press charges. Will you notify Detective Randolph that I want to talk to him?"

Officer Johnson nodded and put his notebook away. "Do you want to call a tow truck?"

"Yes, but I will take care of it." I turned and walked back into the house.

It took thirty-five minutes for the tow truck from Hooper's Garage to show, but no matter. Our family had used them for years. I knew that they would take good care of my Volvo.

Joe Hooper quickly changed the tires and declared that I didn't need a tow. While I sat on the porch waiting for the garage, the outside temperature rose at least 20 degrees. I decided to change clothes and have a salad for supper. It was too hot now for Anthony's Italian sauce.

The minute I walked into the hall I knew something was wrong. Maxie was howling and racing up and down the hall, in and out of the study. She wasn't hurt but seemed upset. I went into the study and glanced at the desk. The Montblanc pen that Aunt Stacy and I had found in the tunnel was gone!

I put Maxie on the desk chair cushion and searched the floor. Perhaps my little furball had knocked the pen off the desk and batted the pen around and under something. I got down on my knees but could only see dust bunnies. Maxie had only been there for a few hours and there was plenty of other stuff for her to play with. She had quickly discovered a long strand of opera pearls that belonged to Great Aunt Liz. For as long as I could remember those pearls hung on the key to the armoire in the back bedroom. I thought there was a story about them, but I couldn't remember it.

My head was spinning with slashed tires. What would I do if this wasn't a safe place to live? I wasn't afraid of a little girl ghost, but I *was* afraid of a person walking through our neighborhood. Someone knocked on the door. I hoped it was Bill—but it wasn't.

Eric stood at the door with a bunch of papers in his hands. I brought him into the study. That seemed to be the best place for meetings except that the Georgian era sofa in the living room was probably full of dust mites.

"Is that the contract to sell the house?" I said. "Aunt Stacy and I have a project and we would like to wait a few weeks before I sign it. If you sold the house tomorrow, we couldn't finish the project."

"What type of project? You all aren't going to change anything. You don't want to invest in this place."

"No. It's nothing like that. Aunt Stacy and I think there may be historical value to this place. She is looking into it."

"Yes, this place is historical but it is still salable. Here, sign on the last page. And I have a few questions for you."

"I'm sorry, Eric, but everything is a mess. Leave the contract with me? I can read it closely overnight and call you tomorrow."

He sighed. "Here. Don't wait too long, though. I have a buyer from Atlanta that is interested. I'll run by tomorrow and get your signed copy." He stood up and started for the door.

At that very moment, Maxie decided to do a crazy-cat run through the room. She yowled, raced around the desk and latched on to the bottom of Eric's pant leg with her tiny sharp claws. He shook his foot, and I leaned over and grabbed her. I don't know why, but I loved that the cat hated Eric.

"Get that damn cat off of me!" he yelled. "You should have left that monster at the vet. This is an expensive suit and if the trousers can't be repaired, I'll send you a bill. Simmons, please just sign the damn contract. I will come by tomorrow."

He slammed the door and headed toward his little red sports

car. It looked new and I thought he must be doing well, but he was pressuring me a little too much for my taste. I sat down at my desk and soothed Maxie while she sat in my lap. Despite his pretty blue eyes, Eric no longer seemed so appealing. On the other hand, Bill hadn't returned my call.

Aunt Stacy would throw a hissy fit when she found out that we didn't have a lot of time to get the old home place registered as historic. I needed to hire a cleaning service to catch the dust bunnies and now new car tires had to be fit into my budget.

Double, double toil and trouble.

I cuddled and rubbed Maxie's head behind her ears and went back into the study. I checked the fridge and realized that it was empty—I would have to go to the Inn for dinner. The best-laid plans of mice and men do often go awry.

10

The doorbell rang and I opened the door. Kate and Joan stood in the shadow of the streetlight—I had forgotten to turn the porch light on.

The day was totally lost after my harrowing experience with slashed tires and by the time I called Joan for dinner reservations at the Inn, I wasn't even sure that I wanted food.

She promised to fix that when she heard my tale of woe. Delectable aromas assaulted my nose as I led us into the kitchen. Joan had brought dinner from the Inn and swung by to pick up Kate on the way.

The kitchen needed work but it wasn't my priority. Michael always joked with our friends that the only reason we had a kitchen in our New York apartment was because it came with it. I shook those thoughts out of my head and listened to what Kate was saying.

"Do you think that granite counter tops are still in vogue?" she asked. I totally ignored that and started pulling our dinner out of the baskets.

Joan responded in my place. "I think that this kitchen should be modernized, but it could be turned into two rooms. What is that in the corner, a pantry by the kitchen table? It should be moved closer to the cooking area," Joan said.

I walked over to the closet and opened the door. It wasn't a pantry. It looked more like an antique pulley with ropes and a slab to sit on. I couldn't recall ever having seen it.

Joan stuck her head inside the closet and clapped her hands in glee. "You have an antique dumbwaiter—the real deal. Kate, stick your head in here."

She peeked in and pointed at the rope. "That rope has been replaced," she said. "I wonder why?"

Joan missed the significance of the statement. "Were you all planning to use this for the fundraiser? It could take a lot of wine glasses up to the third floor. Simmons, I bet you haven't gained an ounce since high school. You have always had the perfect figure. Sit yourself in here and let's see if it still goes up and down."

Kate just stood there. I guess she thought I would protest, but I didn't. It would probably give Aunt Stacy more of a reason not to sell, but we still needed to know if the mansion had been a stop on the Underground Railroad. This might make it more certain.

I slid myself onto the slab and pulled up my knees, and Joan slammed the door. Instantly, the same musty smell Aunt Stacy and I had noticed in the tunnel penetrated my nostrils. I jerked on the rope and then the dumbwaiter started downward and suddenly into a free fall that resembled a carnival ride, finally landing on solid earth. I was in the tunnel.

I couldn't tell exactly what part of the tunnel I was in, but I thought I was about halfway through it, close to where Aunt Stacy and I had found the pen. If so, then this was the perfect escape!

Joan tugged on the rope and the slab began to rise. Ideas were swirling through my mind, but I would have to do more exploration before I told Aunt Stacy. The goose bumps that always gave me something to think about ran down my spine.

I was soon back on the level where Joan and Kate were standing. "That was some ride," I said, not mentioning the tunnel. "It could work for hauling food to the third floor, but it is a unique feature of this old place. Unfortunately, another selling point for Eric."

Kate shook her head. "I'm not sure I would trust him to sell to a residential buyer. He has made his money selling high rise condo developments in larger cities."

Joan spread the food across the table, and I poured us wine. "Do I really want to try to keep up this place?" I asked. "I don't even know if I can afford the yardman. Oh, I forgot to ask Eric who it is."

"I meant to tell you that Margaret and Myrtle both told me that this place didn't have a yardman," Kate said. "We asked the Garden Club to come over and help us get ready for the fundraiser. By the way, we can coordinate all of this at the board meeting. Max's aunt is going to join us and help plan the memorial."

I drew in a deep breath and changed the subject. "Let's talk about the murders. I am torn between selling this place and keeping it." Joan put her glass down and Kate stared at me like I had three heads. "I am serious. It could take forever for the murders to be solved. Can't we at least talk about it?"

"What's to talk about?" Kate asked. "We know that no one on the board did it and I'm sure that Bill is following any leads from his investigation."

"Could the killer think I know something? My tires were

slashed today. Would it be silly to think that the killer slashed my tires to warn me to stay away from this house?"

"Why would this house have anything to do with your tires?" Joan asked. "Yes, Max was killed here, but that doesn't mean anything."

"You're right. I am a lousy detective. I think that the yardman did it and we don't even have a yardman." We all laughed.

We finished eating and talked for a few minutes until I yawned. Kate cleaned up the table. Joan packed everything back in her baskets. After washing and drying the plates and putting them away, they left with promises to get in touch the next day.

After locking up, I walked through the downstairs and started turning off lights. I heard a soft meow as I started for the steps. Maxie blinked up at me and I folded her into my arms.

I thought about how relaxing it would be to spend the night in a king-sized bed in the master bedroom. Maybe I would take a nice cool shower. It was after nine o'clock and still in the eighties outside.

Before I reached the landing of the second floor, I heard heavy pounding on the front door. That brass locker had been there since the door was hung. Uncle Hugh would get Thomas, his butler, to polish that door knocker every day.

I tiptoed to the door and looked through the peep hole. Bill was standing there. His white shirt sleeves were rolled up and he had a slight frown on his face. I cracked the door and peered at him.

"Good evening," he said. He acted as if this was a normal social call. The frown had been replaced with a smile, but he looked tired.

I brought him into the kitchen. Maxie followed us and Bill

reached down and picked her up. She nestled into the crook of his arm. Then he sat down at the table and put her in his lap. She curled up and started purring.

Without asking, I got a plate and the evenings leftovers out of the fridge and set them on the table. He grabbed the plate and reached for the fork. After several bites he gave me a huge thanks and put his fork down. "I was worried about you," he said. "I finally got to the pile of reports on my desk. I saw about the tire slashing incident."

"Your Officer Johnson thinks it was kids in the neighborhood. Do you?" I asked. "Don't say it is too early to tell."

We both laughed. "It is highly likely," he said. "A mailbox down the street got bashed and someone threw rotten tomatoes on a neighbor's porch, but the neighbor didn't see a thing."

"Have you questioned the neighbors about Max's murder? A neighbor could have slipped across the street before the meeting." At his frown, I let my sentence trail off. Besides, most of my neighbors were at least seventy years old, and none of them had a reason to kill the Everharts. I didn't even remember who lived there except that Maddie Taylor's mother had grown up in that house. I wondered if Maddie knew anything about part of the Underground Railroad running through this area.

Suddenly I knew the tears were coming. I put my head in my hands and heaved a huge sigh. Bill got up from the table and engulfed me in a big bear hug. I noted that the smell of his aftershave was nice. I leaned back and looked into his warm brown eyes.

I let the moment pass. So did he. He dropped his hands and stepped away. He was doing his job and simply got carried away.

I sat back down and took a sip of wine. "I keep suspecting everyone of murder. Are you making any progress? Anything you want to share?"

Bill shook his head. "This is one of the hardest cases I have ever worked. There are too many suspects. We *do* know that Veronica wasn't on the road near McBee when Max was murdered. She changed her mind about leaving earlier for her movie shoot. She wanted to explain to Max's Aunt Mary why she was leaving him and had booked a flight out of the airport in Greer for later.

"Max owed his aunt money and Veronica wanted her to know that she would pay her back as soon as she had money from the movie and that it would be a substantial amount. It seems that Max had invested in some kind of development scheme in New York, and it turned out to be a Ponzi scheme."

I rolled my eyes. "So now, as suspects, we have the entire Rhett Street Troupe, anyone in this neighborhood, disgruntled actors from New York, and maybe an angry investor who helped Max start the Ponzi scheme?"

"I am following the evidence that we have," he said. "I am thinking about what it might all mean, but I haven't come up with any definite answers. Kate told me that Max's aunt is coming down for the board meeting. She wants to talk to you and Kate and try to help the theater raise money."

Bill took his plate to the sink. "I told Johnson that I would ride through your neighborhood with him tonight and help look for joy riders and tire slashers. Do you mind if I leave my car in your driveway? It will be quicker for me to get home from here. That way, Johnson won't have to take me back to the station."

"I will leave the porch light on for you. It would probably be safer to leave it on anyway." I reached out to touch his arm, but he was already at the front door. A marked police car was waiting for him out front. I waved and he waved back as the car pulled away.

I started up the stairs with Maxie on my heels. I turned and talked to her. "I thought you didn't like men. You certainly liked Bill Randolph. He *is* nice on the eyes, isn't he?" Maxie meowed in response.

I reached the second landing and felt the buzz of my phone in my pocket. It was Aunt Stacy. I panicked a little—she grew up in the age of the Beatles and was spry for her age, but she felt more like my grandmother than my father's sister. She usually went to bed around nine and it was after 9:30. "Do I need to call an ambulance? Have you fallen?"

"Don't be ridiculous," she said. "One of your neighbors just woke me up because she saw Bill Randolph's car there. She had the nerve to ask me if he planned to spend the night. If you are courting that nice fellow, maybe you all should be more discreet."

"Bill left his car here. He's out with a patrol officer trying to find the teenagers that slashed my tires. Do you want me to have a friendly word with the neighbors? I'm not even sure what 'courting' means. Why don't you call and tell her to sit up and watch Bill's car? She can tell us who did it if his tires get slashed."

11

The next week seemed to go faster than a roller coaster that was out of control. Maxie and I spent most days getting ourselves acclimated to the mansion and the neighborhood.

I didn't hear from Bill or Kate. I assumed he was working on the murders and Kate was distracted by the agenda for the board meeting. Although I was living at McBee now, I had said that the board could still meet there. People from all over the country had come for the Rosemont Festival and Joan had had an influx of visitors at the Inn, but the festival would be over by then.

I left Maxie in the cool of our bedroom and walked down the hill to Main Street. It had been years since I had been to Rosemont's Summertime Festival. Large white tents lined both sides of the street. The sun beat down on top of the tents and I heard the roar of window fans as I approached a booth.

Shelia, from the theater, was standing in the booth selling handmade jewelry. Lots of colored bead necklaces hung from wire that ran across the length of the tent in a most pleasing rainbow effect. I moved closer to look at it all. Shelia had taken a turquoise necklace off the wire and was showing it to an admiring customer.

I heard a familiar voice behind me. "I think you've met my sister," said Bill. He came into the booth with two cold beers in his hands. His sister reached out and took hers.

I turned to the woman and smiled. "No, I don't need an introduction. I remember you from our time together at Rosemont High," I said. "Lucy, isn't it?"

"That's right. Simmons, I have a prom picture of you and Bill. Our mother insisted on having it on top of the piano with the rest of our family pictures. You haven't changed a bit."

I didn't know if I should say thank you or "You must be kidding," so I didn't say anything.

"Lucy came down to see family this week," said Bill. "We went rafting on the Chattooga yesterday. It was a great way to cool off in this sweltering heat."

Shelia still held the turquoise necklace in her hand. She looked eagerly from Lucy to Bill. Lucy looked at the necklace. Bill took my arm and pulled me away from the booth.

"I have invited myself to the board meeting," he said. "I need one last look at each member. Kate said she thought it was a good idea and would add me to the agenda."

"You mean to put us all in my dining room like it's an Agatha Christie novel? If you can name the killer, then I am all for anything that you can do."

"The board thinks that I am there to supply security services for the gala in Max's honor. I need to see what the board has in mind for this gala. Let's hope we have the killer in custody by then."

Lucy came out of the tent. "Bill, I bought the necklace," she said. "I knew you would like it. Turquoise is a symbol for personal protection and your favorite gem. It's your birthstone too." She grabbed him by the elbow. "Come on, let's go down by the river and enjoy the music. It will be much cooler by the falls."

Bill waved goodbye to me, and I watched them walk toward the falls. I turned around to admire Shelia's jewelry. The perfect pair of turquoise earrings caught my eye. "Did you craft these? They are exquisite."

She nodded. "I've been making jewelry since I got a kit in fifth grade. It started as a hobby and has turned into a full-time business. I even have a site on Etsy now."

12

The hot August sun cast shadows across the wide expanse of the lawn at McBee Mansion. I stood at the door and invited each of the board members to come in and join us. Max's Aunt Mary had arrived a few minutes before and was seated at the dining table beside Kate who was looking at a pile of notes in front of her. Everyone seemed antsy—Eric kept hopping up and down to get water and tea for everyone.

As soon as I walked into the room, I swore I got a whiff of that musty aromatic odor that had been in the tunnel. The aroma was faint and no one else seemed to notice. *I certainly can't go around sniffing behind everyone's ears*, I thought. The smell must be seeping into the room from the walls of this old mansion.

I pulled out the nineteenth-century Queen Anne chair next to Joan and let my eyes wander around the room. *Did one on these people kill Max and Veronica and think they could get away with it?*

The front door opened and closed, and Bill burst into the room. "Sorry. I got held up at the office," he said.

"Did you mean for that to be a pun?" I asked. Everyone laughed.

Kate cleared her throat. "We are all here. Let's get started."

Margaret Sellers raised her hand "Isn't it disrespectful to have a fundraiser at this time?"

Clearly everyone had a different opinion. At least three people talked at once. Kate banged her gavel and I winced at the new mark it probably made on my antique table. "There's someone here who can answer that question," she said.

Kate introduced Max's Aunt Mary and asked her to speak to the cause. She stood up and gave an excellent, passionate speech. Her idea for our event was more of a memorial than a fundraiser. "Of course, we will ask everyone in New York to contribute to the Rhett Street Players in honor of Max. It will be a donation."

Kate nodded. "The board will also ask for contributions toward the memorial. I don't think that we should ask for people to buy tickets."

"And just how do you propose we finance this memorial?" asked Myrtle in a haughty voice. "We will need to have the garden party with wine and lots of good food. We will need to put on a magnificent spread in that great actor's honor and that will be very expensive."

Aunt Mary glanced at Myrtle and then back at the rest of us. "I will pay for the expenses to give my only nephew—and Veronica—a great party and memorial service in order to honor them."

I felt the sun through the windows overlooking the dining room. Dust motes floated through the air. My contribution to this affair was making the house and grounds available. I yawned and tried to act like I was paying attention. My eyes scanned the room. These people had come together to help the theater. If one of them were a killer, why would they target Max and Veronica? Wouldn't the killer have an agenda against one of the local board members? I had learned from reading lots of mystery plays that a killer needed motive, opportunity, and means in order to be successful. One of my favorites was *Arsenic and Old Lace*. It was a well-executed play. I hoped I could write one as good.

"Don't you agree, Simmons?" Kate said.

I jumped as if I had been stabbed by the dagger. "Of course, I think it is a great idea."

"You think that it is a good idea to honor Veronica too or it is a good idea to not honor her?"

Aunt Mary stood up again. "It was Max's idea to help Simmons and the theater. Veronica wasn't happy about doing this. Do all of you know that she was coming to Highlands to tell me that she was leaving Max? She knew that Max had lost all of their money in a Ponzi Scheme. She wanted *me* to give her a lump sum of money to go quietly away."

For the first time in my experience with the Theater Board, it was quiet enough to hear the dust motes floating in the air. I needed to address this issue.

"In light of what we have learned today, I want to honor Max," I said. "Although he obviously had some problems, he was sincere about helping our theater. I am sure Veronica's family will honor her memory in a thoughtful way. I move that we make this a memorial to Max Everhart and call it that. Any donations to the celebration in his memory will go to the Rhett Street Players."

The motion passed without any dissension. I could tell that Kate was relieved. "Everyone has their committee assignments. Simmons, I want you to be in charge of letting the people in New York know about this memorial. Maybe get his agent to put an announcement in the *New York Times*. Instead of ticket sales, we will ask for donations to the theater in Max's name. Let's hope we raise enough to have a great production season. We will meet next week to finalize plans." She banged the gavel. "The meeting is adjourned." Chairs slid away from the table. The 12 x 14-foot rug that Grandfather found in a bazaar in Turkey muffled the sound.

I started toward the kitchen to put glasses in the dishwasher and Eric came up behind me. "Have you signed the contract to sell? I may have buyers that want to look at the property next week. I've had a number of people who have lost interest in the past few weeks thanks to you. We can have dinner this week and discuss it." His shiny blue eyes smiled at me, but I'd begun to get a different feeling from them than I had when I'd first seen him. Besides, he obviously didn't like cats.

"I don't know what to say, Eric," I said. "I am not as ready to sell but I don't know exactly why I feel this way. I think I should wait until after the memorial to make a decision. It would be hard to show the place *and* prepare for a party, don't you think?"

Maxie meowed and Eric jumped. "There's that damn cat. I am getting out of here before it attacks me and destroys my clothes." Maxie sashayed to her water bowl and I giggled.

Joan had left the meeting early and came rushing back with Jim and enough pizza from the Swamp Rabbit Cafe to feed an army. Kate and Jackson wandered in from the dining room and we all sat at the kitchen table. Jim poured wine and water for everyone.

This amazed me. We had had a pizza night without any planning! This would never have happened in New York!

We were just getting started when Bill hurried in.

"Sorry," he said, looking at me. "Sergeant thinks he has a lead on the vandals and needs your slashed tires if you still have them."

"Are you any closer to finding the killer? Don't tell me it is early times. You have had plenty of time to interview and follow leads."

With a mouthful of pizza, Bill kept the smile on his face, but shook his head. I took a bite of the wood-fired pizza and I understood. The Swamp used locally-grown ingredients and farm-fresh veggies. It was enough to take your mind off everything.

Kate wiped her mouth and proceeded to give us her theory about the murders. "It's obvious that it has to be someone with an old vendetta against Max. That means it must be someone from New York. I don't believe it is really a crazed actor. There are more than eight million crazy actors and that is a lot of suspects."

"I tried to watch all of the board members during the meeting," said Joan. "None of them acted suspiciously to me. It was amazing that such a diverse group could agree on anything. The board did seem happy that I would donate some of the refreshments and try to get some of our restaurants to contribute."

I nodded my head. "It was great to have Aunt Mary come and explain the situation with Veronica and announce she's paying for the party," I said. "Do y'all think that the same person that killed Max killed Veronica?"

"Of course," said Jackson. "It was Veronica's lover that killed Max. Then he had to kill Veronica because…Wait a minute. I'm an investment broker. This has got to be about money. If Max had lost all his money and Veronica was after money, then maybe her lover really *did* kill him. Maybe they argued and this guy picked up the dagger and stabbed Max."

"I see a bunch of holes in that theory," I said. "First, how did this guy get to McBee Mansion? Did he come with Veronica? If he was Veronica's lover, why would he kill *her*?"

"Stop!" said Bill. A hush fell over the room. "This isn't a mystery game. We aren't playing Clue. These are real people. All of you could be in danger if the murderer finds out that you all are trying to solve this crime. I suggest that you go about planning the memorial and leave crime solving to me."

The front door slammed, and I heard Aunt Stacy calling me from the hall. Before I could even get out of my chair, she blew into the room. She was wearing her pearls, which she only wore to serious meetings. "I need to talk to you. Eric Loftis and Maude Ledbetter are with me."

I invited them all to sit down and Bill pulled up more chairs. I offered plates and glasses. Eric grabbed a piece of pizza, but Maude sat with her hands folded in her lap.

Aunt Stacy continued. "Since Maude is the Vice President of the Rosemont Historical Society, I brought her over to see the tunnel. We are going to work together to get it on the register. Eric was showing a condo and saw me picking Maude up to come over here. He is going to help us with this project. We will leave you to your party and go look at the tunnel."

Bill stood up. "I'll come with you. I haven't had a chance to see all of it."

The four hurried out and I looked around the table at my remaining friends. "What tunnel?" said Kate.

"It's probably nothing but hard compacted dirt," I whispered, "but I hope we can find something historical about it."

Kate and Jackson both nodded. Jim's phone rang and he excused himself. Joan and I cleaned up the kitchen and I left a couple of pieces of pizza for Eric. I waved at all of them as they pulled away from the house. All was quiet, considering all the moans and groans that a mansion of this size has.

I looked down at my iPhone. The four had been gone more than thirty minutes so I thought they were done. I started locking up the house but heard noises. Aunt Stacy and Eric came back into the kitchen just before I locked the dead bolt. "We may have found something," Aunt Stacy announced. Eric grabbed a slice of cold pizza.

"We called Maude's husband and he met us at the end of the tunnel with a shovel and a metal detector. There's something metal at the other end of the tunnel but it was too late and too dark for us to see. We are going to work on it tomorrow. Don't let us bother you if we get here early."

I wrapped the rest of the pizza in aluminum foil for Eric and sent them on their way. It was obvious that he wanted to stay, but Aunt Stacy put her arm in his and pulled him to the front door.

I groaned to myself. I had planned to sleep late, but they would probably be here before eight. I had also planned to have a word with Bill because I wanted to know his impression of the board.

I climbed the stairs to bed and a Shakespeare quote ran through my head. *Innocent sleep. Sleep that soothes away all our worries. Sleep that puts each day to rest. Sleep that relieves the weary laborer and heals hurt minds. Sleep, the main course in life's feast, and the most nourishing.*

13

I felt Maxie pawing my head. It had become her way of waking me up when she wanted attention. I glanced at the clock. Nine twenty. I had slept late but the most amazing thing was that I hadn't had a nightmare—I was finally adjusting to my new life in Rosemont. Today I would set up my office.

I was excited about finally getting to work on my first play. A workshop in Iowa had been helpful in getting me started and I was sure this winter would be the perfect time to do it. But the phone rang before my feet hit the floor. *The best laid plans…*

Eric was talking before I even got the phone to my ear. "I've got a hot prospect. Take that crazed cat and get out for the morning. I think you will be happy if the two of you can agree on a price."

I sighed. "I will let you show it this morning, Eric, but I'm not putting it on the market until after Max's memorial. I'll go over to Kate's. Call me after you are done."

It took a quick shower and threw on some clothes. I grabbed Maxie and went to the car. Had I left dishes in the sink? Too late for that, I thought, as I pulled out of the driveway. I hadn't even had time to make a cup of coffee.

Kate lived close by in another neighborhood where the houses had historical value. These beauties never went on the market—most were left to the next generation. For instance, Kate had lived in the same house all of her life. She had spent four years at Converse College, married Ted, and they'd moved back to her old home place. Although Ted left three years later, Kate had stayed.

I walked up the path to her back door. Maxie was squirming, ready to get out of my arms. Kate opened the door and stuck a steaming cup of Maxwell House into my outstretched hand. Now, that's a true friend, I thought. Maxie ran into her den, jumped on her sofa and promptly curled up and went to sleep. We settled at her kitchen table.

"Are you okay?" she said. "It's awfully early for you to be dressed and about."

I explained about Eric still being fired up to sell McBee. "He's showing the place this morning and I don't even know if I want to sell. What is wrong with me?"

Kate patted my arm. "Nothing. You have had too many extraordinary things happen to you since you left New York. Give yourself time. Don't let Eric or anyone else push you." She sipped her coffee. "Until we find a home, I am thinking that the Rhett Street Players could rent your third floor for rehearsals and readings. Think about that. It could help you pay the light bill."

A wave of relief washed over me. "Kate, you are wonderful. I will give that a lot of thought." I rifled through my purse for my phone. "And I will call Max's agent and try to get him to put the memorial service for Max in the *New York Times* like you asked me to."

Kate went into her office, and I sat in the den on the sofa next to Maxie. She stretched and rearranged herself, her tail flopping on my leg. Max's agent, Don Heath, answered on the second ring. I had met him on several occasions.

"Simmons!" he said. "This is a horrible tragedy. We closed the office in honor of Max. But I had some catching up to do. I came in early this morning. I am devastated. Max was a wonderful client. High strung when he was directing—he was a perfectionist."

"I agree, but that is what made him great."

"What can I do for you?"

I explained about our plans for the memorial. Don was more than agreeable. "I will get the notice of the memorial in the *Times* and contact as many of our friends as possible. Of course, I will be there."

"One more question, Don. Do you think that someone from Max's past could have killed him?" It was a blunt question, but Don had never minced words.

"A detective called and asked me the same question a few days ago." He paused. "You remember that when Max finished rehearsals, he gave notes to everybody—and they were always negative. He would even criticize an actor's breathing. No one was exempt. The entire cast and crew always hated him. And then the show would win a Tony and the cast would suddenly love him. That was Max."

I gave Don more detail about the memorial service and he promised again to get the word out. Before we said our good-byes, he suggested I call the 42nd Street Theater and get everyone there in on it. There were a lot of publications that would be happy to run an announcement for Max's memorial service, he said.

Kate came in with another cup of coffee and a large slice of banana bread. "How'd that go?

"Max's agent is on board. I think he and some of Max's friends will fly down in their private plane. He had no clue that anyone would want to hurt Max." I shrugged. "The reason for the murder must be local. Someone here must've done it."

"Ridiculous. Rosemont is a quiet law-abiding town. It isn't an all-hell-break-loose wild west or a massive criminal-riddled city. We will probably never know what happened."

"Well, I hope Bill keeps at it and gets a break in the case, but it needs to be soon." I took a deep breath. "Don reminded me that Max could always pull out the most amazing performances even from mediocre actors. Broadway will miss him." Hopefully, many would come to the memorial.

"Have you talked to anyone at 42nd Street?"

"As a matter of fact, that's my next call. Don suggested that too." I took a bite of the warm banana bread and punched in the numbers. After working there for ten years, it would be a while before I forgot the phone number.

The box office volunteer answered on the second ring, and we chatted for a few minutes. "The theater is dark today, but there's always someone here to check on props and sets every day." When I told the volunteer about the memorial, she told me Max's Aunt Mary had already called and she had turned the information over to the publicity manager.

"Really," I said.

The volunteer paused. "Simmons, do you remember a night a few years ago when you entertained people from Rosemont that came to New York? I believe there were theater people from Greenville too. You wore yourself out trying to entertain them and run the show at the same time. It was really funny because they expected you to give them orchestra seats. *Give* being the operative word."

I felt a jolt in my brain. People from Rosemont *had* met Max that week. I had taken them backstage and introduced them to him and the stage crew. They'd met Patrick Stewart and most of the cast and afterwards, we all went out for drinks on Theater Row. I was almost positive that Max had joined us then too.

I thanked the volunteer and hung up the phone. Who had been on that trip? Aunt Stacy was part of that entourage. She would know.

I punched in her number, but no one answered. She had a cell phone, but was always losing it. Then I remembered that she had told me she was meeting the Ledbetters at the tunnel. I said goodbye to Kate, grabbed Maxie, and headed toward where the tunnel ended.

Sure enough, there they were, sitting on the ground outside the tiny opening of the tunnel, covered in mud. Maude's husband Ralph was standing off to the side. I hopped out of the car and heard them arguing before I even got near.

Maude was shouting. "There is absolutely no proof whatsoever that this was used for Underground Railroad or anything else worthwhile in the history of Rosemont."

"Just because we didn't find any proof this morning doesn't mean it isn't here," yelled Aunt Stacy.

Maude was indignant. "I wouldn't put it past you to hide something here and then look surprised when a silver spoon you bought on Amazon turned up. You certainly wouldn't use any of your own sterling."

Aunt Stacy scooped up a pile of mud in her hand. She wouldn't dare throw it, would she? I stepped in between them. I could only imagine what was going through their minds.

Both women eventually calmed down. "It would probably be more profitable to research what was happening at McBee Mansion during Prohibition," said Maude. "Don't you think that homemade spirits could have been carted through the tunnel and sent downstream to Savannah or Charleston? Wouldn't that qualify as historical value? If you found bottles of the era, that would be proof. I suspect that you need to use the Geiger counter and go through the whole tunnel."

Aunt Stacy nodded. "That can be a project for another day. We need to get cleaned up."

I could see the gratitude on Ralph Ledbetter's face. I am sure he hadn't wanted to break up a mudslinging contest between two determined Southern ladies.

I grabbed Aunt Stacy's arm and pointed her toward the car. "I've been trying to find you. I need some help." I grabbed some plastic from the trunk and put it down on the passenger seat. "First, though you need to get a shower."

Aunt Stacy was pensive on the way to the Woodlands. "I always knew that Maude was hard to deal with, but I can't believe that she was so nasty about my idea about the Underground Railroad. She's the one who would bury something and then act surprised. I will keep an eye on her from now on." She paused. "What is it that I can help you with? You aren't in trouble, are you?"

"No, we can talk about it at lunch."

It took over an hour for Aunt Stacy to shower and change. She was happy living in the retirement community and had lots of friends—and she felt the need to talk to everyone she met. When she finally got to me in reception, I stood and grabbed her elbow. "Would you like to eat at the club or would you prefer a restaurant. We could go to the Chop House. Their burgers are great," I said.

"The club is fine. It won't be crowded and we can have a quiet visit. I know how hard this has all been for you. Readjusting to Rosemont *and* losing your friend Max."

I hugged my aunt as we walked into the club. Sam, who had worked at the club since he was sixteen years old, was seating a group in front of us. We got a table for two by a floor-to-ceiling window. The view was magnificent if you ignored the old codgers riding golf carts across a perfectly landscaped 15th hole.

Once we were served drinks, I jumped right in. "What do you remember about the trip to New York that you took with the Rhett Street Players Board and the Greenville Theater group?"

She put her glass of chardonnay down and smirked at me. "Well, I sprained my ankle getting out of a taxi in front of the hotel. Eric Loftis helped me get to my room. I was sharing with Maddie, and I had to wear horrid shoes to dinner." She laughed. "Let's see. It was the next night that we came to the 42nd to see you." She thought for a minute. "I remember that Max joined us after the show. I don't think Veronica was with him then. Anyway, we all had a lovely time. I really appreciated the job you did for the theater group."

"Do you remember who else was there? Any of the Rhett Street Board?"

Aunt Stacy's attention wandered. "Look. There's Eric at the bar. And isn't that a nice-looking gentleman with him?" She shouted to him across the restaurant and everyone in the room turned around. Most people smiled and waved when they saw who it was.

Eric came rushing over. "Robert Taylor is interested in your property. I showed the property to a development group this morning. When I told Robert about it he said he would like to see it. I can call and get him to meet me there this afternoon."

"No," said Aunt Stacy. "This isn't the proper time to discuss business. I want to know if you remember our trip to New York."

"Of course. The whole Greenville Theater board went. We had a great time. Didn't we have drinks and dinner at Sardi's? I still crave their grilled filet mignon medallions. Great time."

"Who else was on that trip?" I asked.

"The whole board. Jackson wasn't on it then, but everybody else. There was this obnoxious fellow from Greenville that kept telling Max how much he liked Max's Aunt Mary. He was a bag of hot air."

"I remember him," said Aunt Stacy. "Olson Bellew. He goes to New York for a Broadway play every year."

Eric looked at his watch. "I have to be back at the office in twenty minutes. Simms, call me when you get back to the mansion." I watched Eric return to the bar and sign his check.

I was back to square one. No suspects. That New York trip had happened years ago. If a Rhett Street Board member or a Greenville Theater board member had wanted to kill Max, it would have happened before now.

After a great lunch and a lot of talk about the Historical Society, Aunt Stacy signed the bill and we walked into the afternoon heat toward my Volvo.

14

Typical of late summer in South Carolina, a late afternoon storm formed dark clouds over McBee Mansion. Thunder rumbled in the distance. Heat waves of at least ninety degrees persisted until three or four in the afternoon. Then thunderstorms followed.

I hurried from the study to the kitchen. I wanted to be prepared if the lights went out. Batteries and flashlights had been at the top of my list when I'd gone to the hardware store a couple of days ago, so all the flashlights were ready to go. I took three.

It felt comfortable to slip into Uncle Hugh's desk chair. I glanced around the room and smiled. I had made some progress in making the mansion more livable. I'd gotten the study clean and in some semblance of order—I had rubbed the desk with a beeswax polish until it shone. I had arranged my playwriting books on top.

The Elizabethan writing desk was beautifully carved and put together with handmade nails—the real deal, as Aunt Stacy had stated. Uncle Hugh claimed it had come from an English ancestor and passed down with the rest of his inheritance. For all I knew, it was an antique, but could have been bought in a warehouse in London on one of his many trips abroad.

The rumble from the approaching storm grew louder and I jumped up to find Maxie. My perfect calico cat was curled in the middle of my four-poster rice bed, another antique that had been in the family for years, acquired during the Civil War era.

The first boom startled Maxie, who didn't like loud noises, and she let out a piercing yowl. The second was even louder, sounding more like a cannon shot than thunder. The whole house shook.

I grabbed the cat and hurried down the steps. On the last one, I turned my ankle and gasped for breath, barely keeping Maxie and me from sprawling on the floor. I sat down on the bottom step and rubbed my foot. Then, suddenly, I heard pounding on the front door. I limped down the hall and opened the door to a crowd of my neighbors. Rain splatters sprinkled on the path to my door.

"Are you okay?" Several voices rose over the din of fire trucks and police sirens. I looked to see more neighbors coming down the street toward me and glanced at the grandfather clock. The hands had moved forward at least thirty minutes from the time that l left the study. Had I blacked out?

"What time is it?" I said.

Aunt Stacy pushed her way through the crowd and gathered me in her arms. "Someone tried to blow you up."

At that news, I burst into tears. Maxie licked my hand and gave me a soft nudge with her head.

"Let's get you inside and have a look at your ankle," said Aunt Stacy. She led me back into the hall and closed the door, then helped me to a seat and then disappeared into a bathroom.

"Nosy neighbors," she said, as she came back down the hallway. "One of them could be the bomber. I didn't see the Ledbetters out there, but I would not put anything past them. She is determined to keep this mansion from getting special attention. Her grandmother wasn't accepted into polite society in the late forties and she hasn't forgiven the McAbees for it." She finished wrapping an Ace bandage around my ankle.

I thought about what she'd said and shook my head. "Aunt Stacy, the Ledbetters would not blow up the mansion. They're preservationists."

I limped back into the study and gasped. Two large holes gaped at me—one in the door of the dumbwaiter, another in the door to the secret passage. And something looked odd about the wall over the fireplace—the quilt was gone. Someone really *had* bombed my home and a thief had stolen my property!

A wave of nausea rumbled through my gut. The reality of the situation hit me, and I tried to take a deep breath as I wiped more tears from my eyes. I looked over at the desk chair and realized that if I hadn't gone to check on Maxie, I would still have been sitting there when the second explosion happened.

A door opened and Bill came rushing into the study. He wrapped his arms around me. "Are you okay? Do we need to get you to the hospital?"

Eric Loftis was right behind him. "How long before we can get this repaired?"

The room went quiet as Bill, Aunt Stacy, and I all turned to him and frowned. Eric shrugged his shoulders. "You look fine, Simmons. The kids in this neighborhood probably set off a potato gun. I played with those when I was a kid." He paused. "I just meant that if we are selling this property, we need to get this fixed."

I ignored him and turned back to Bill. "I'm okay. Let's put ice on my ankle and I'll sit here for a while." Aunt Stacy charged off to the kitchen and Bill sat down in a chair next to me. Eric disappeared, mumbling something about finding a carpenter that worked for his development company.

Once everyone else had trickled from the house, I turned to Bill. "You don't think it was kids having a good time, do you? Is this connected with the murders somehow?"

"I don't know, but I *do* think someone wants to scare you. Simms, how many people know about the tunnel? Maybe something is hidden—buried—in there and someone wants you and Stacy to back off before you find it."

"I will never back off," said Aunt Stacy, who was standing in the doorway holding a bag of frozen peas. "The McBees have always stood their ground. When I married James McBee, I learned the family code. I will never let anyone take advantage of us or scare us into retreating from anything."

"Could she be a target too?" I asked, stopping to think. "I don't know how anyone knows about the tunnel other than Maude Ledbetter. Aunt Stacy and Maude almost had a little mudslinging over whether our idea about the Underground Railroad made sense, but Maude certainly would not resort to a potato gun."

Sergeant Johnson from the police department appeared in the doorway. "Pipe bomb," he said. "Not a potato gun. It was a pipe bomb. The culprit dropped it and ran. Forensics is checking it for fingerprints, but I doubt there will be any. Those teenage hooligans do need to be caught, though. They destroyed another mailbox last night."

The officer pointed toward the blown door into the tunnel. "Do you mind if we take a look in there?"

I shook my head. "Go ahead." Bill followed his sergeant into the tunnel. Seconds later, both came barreling out.

"It's too dangerous for us to dig through the dirt," said the officer.

I looked at Bill. He nodded in agreement with the sergeant. "We need to board up both ends and wait until the earth has settled."

"No matter what, I am planning to stay with Simmons until life is back to normal," said Aunt Stacy. I had always thought of her as my grandmother and once again, in her old-fashioned Southern way, she was trying to protect me.

I heard noises in the hallway and looked up to see Joan with a basket full of food and Kate carrying a box of chocolates and a bottle of wine. I fought back tears. I had friends who really cared, but my tears were from something else. I had inherited this mansion, but I was suddenly unsure that I had inherited the McBee gumption. Uncle Hugh had entrusted me with the care of this place. Did I want to sell my family's history? Could I afford to keep up this huge responsibility?

Bill shook me and brought me back to reality. "Simms, are you okay? I thought that you had drifted off. Do you want to go to the hospital? Maybe we should get you checked out. Maybe you have a concussion." He sat down on a stool next to me and looked into my teary eyes.

A wave of adrenaline washed over me, and I suddenly felt my confidence return. "No, I'm fine. And I am not going to let a little thing like a pipe bomb scare me into selling this place. There's a reason that someone wants me to leave and I'm going to find out why."

"You are trying to solve Max's murder, so maybe whoever did it wants you dead too," said Bill. "But this may not have anything to do with the murders. Finding out is *my* job. I am working on it. Don't get in the middle of something dangerous."

I threw up my arms. "How dangerous can it be to talk to the people that were here for a board meeting? I have walked from one end of Manhattan to the other end at night. That was much scarier living there than in Rosemont."

"That's my girl," Aunt Stacy said. "You remind me of Scarlett when she ripped the curtains off the wall. You are as spunky as I thought you were."

"Scarlett O'Hara?" Joan said. She placed steaming dishes of lasagna, crusty bread, and a bowl of mixed greens on the kitchen table.

"Scarlett was before your time," Aunt Stacy said as she sat down at one end of the table and I at the other. Everyone found a place and Aunt Stacy said a blessing. After the "Amen," she looked around the table. "I'm also thankful that we can stay here while Bill and his men investigate."

I looked around. These people had all been here when I needed them. I wasn't hungry, but I needed their companionship. I moved my food around with my fork.

All I wanted was to write my play and build a new life in Rosemont. If someone was trying to stop me, I would make it hard for them. I didn't think that a murderer would be dumb enough to fire a pipe bomb at the house. I would get to the bottom of it and leave the murder-solving to Bill. I looked over at him. He was taking hearty bites from his full plate.

Eric barged into the dining room, grabbed a plate, and sat down. Joan looked at him and then at me. "Did you find a carpenter to repair the damage?" I asked. "There's not any hurry."

Eric gulped down his food. "He can't come until next week. The sergeant told me that they had boarded it up. I'll make sure to check on it. Don't forget that I have some prospects who will want to see it."

Quiet settled and the only sound was the clinking of utensils. Every plate was almost clean when Eric jumped up. "I hate to eat and run, but I have a conference call with clients in New York. Thanks for dinner." He waved as he went out of the door.

Joan shook her head. "Of all the nerve...he is a real piece of work. I thought he would be an asset when I told Kate to ask him to be on the board, but he's been nothing but a nuisance. I hope he doesn't think he can turn up every night for a free meal." She shrugged her shoulders. "Then again, he *does* bring clients to the Inn and they spend a lot of money. I shouldn't complain. I know that he's young and works hard. He will sell this place and get a good deal for you, Simms."

"Don't worry," I said. "I am not going to be intimidated into selling the mansion. No one can scare me into making a decision that I am not ready to make. I know I keep seesawing about living here or buying a condo. I am going to call my accountant and find out what kind of budget I would need to maintain this place."

At my pronouncement, the dining room table exploded with cheers and hoorays. I hadn't realized how much everyone wanted McBee Mansion to continue to be lived in by a McBee. Aunt Stacy beamed. Grinning, I stood up but pain shot up my leg. I quickly sat back down, but once the pain diminished, Bill and Kate helped me up the stairs and waited outside while I changed into my sleepy pants. I eased myself into bed and called to them. We talked for a minute and then Kate hugged me. Bill patted me on the shoulder and then they left.

I closed my eyes and felt Maxie curl up at top of my head. What seemed like a few minutes passed and I looked at the clock. It was three in the morning! I had drifted off and slept for almost five hours.

It was time for more Tylenol—my ankle was throbbing with pain. I crept out of bed and slowly got myself to the stairs with Maxie right behind me. She continued to act more like a dog than a cat.

Despite the pain, I put each foot down with determination. I grabbed the banister and slowly made my way down the steps and into the kitchen. I would not be intimidated by someone trying to force me to leave the mansion.

I drank a glass of water and was putting it in the drainer beside the sink when Aunt Stacy wandered into the kitchen.

"Did you hear that noise?" she said.

"No, what?"

"A loud creak?"

About that time, something slammed against the house. I looked at Aunt Stacy and then limped over to the phone and dialed 911.

15

Bill arrived before the patrol car. He had on pressed khakis and a light brown polo that matched his eyes. Although it was still the middle of the night, the whiskers on his face were gone—he looked like we had called him away from an important engagement or a date.

Aunt Stacy had made tea and I was sipping a decaf nighttime version. My tee shirt screamed "I am Woman. Hear me roar." I could see the amusement in Bill's eyes.

He headed for the tunnel and discovered that the door had been pried open and a pile of dirt was in front of it. The noise we had heard was the door and not a breaking window. At least that was a blessing.

I could feel tears coming and tried to make myself look as if I would roar. "Is someone trying to kill us?" I said. "I hope that helps you find this crazy person."

Bill returned to the kitchen. "Both of you think about what you have been doing lately. Have you done anything to anyone in the neighborhood?"

I thought for a moment. "Well, I understand that some in the area are afraid I will sell to a developer—no one in the Historical District seems to want that. You'd think they would tell me, though, and not just try to scare me off." The tears in my eyes weren't helping with the printing on my shirt. I certainly didn't feel a roar coming on. I was scared and felt like my life was out of control.

Aunt Stacy chimed in. "I have been dealing with the Historical Society since we discovered the tunnel. I wouldn't put anything past the Ledbetters. Since I showed them the tunnel, they keep calling me." She thought for a moment and continued. "I don't think they would really try to harm us, but they could sabotage the mansion and keep us from getting on the Historical Register." She looked at Bill. "Have you talked to them since the pipe bomb? That seems like the most logical explanation."

"No, but I have several people to talk to at the moment. A car will be on patrol here for the rest of the night. Both of you go back to bed and try to get some sleep. We will talk in the morning."

Bill closed his notebook and I hobbled to the stairs. Before I could take the first step, he was at my side. "I think payback time has arrived." I looked into his eyes. "Lean on me," he said, "and I will help you up the steps. It's the least I can do to compensate for all the time you followed me around the golf course. I always had a better score when you were around."

We made it to the top of the steps and I leaned in and hugged him. I felt a strong hug in return. That was enough for the moment. "Please find the killer and let us turn our lives back to normal."

"I promise," he said. I hobbled to my bed and listened to his footsteps softly treading down the steps.

I slept in fits and starts. At 6 a.m., I finally gave up and tried to hop out of bed. My ankle was less swollen and the pain had receded, but I instantly remembered the happenings during the night. I smelled coffee and realized that Aunt Stacy was already in the kitchen. I washed my face, brushed my teeth, and threw on jeans and my favorite tee. I would be home all day and expected it to be a normal day of peace and quiet. I also hoped that it would be the day that Bill found Max's killer.

Aunt Stacy set a plate of French toast made with honey and orange extract in front of me. She had decorated my plate with a couple of orange slices and a piece of bacon. At seven, the doorbell rang, and she went to answer the door. Waves of laughter drifted from the hall.

Kate, Shelia, and Matt came bounding into the room. Aunt Stacy put more plates on the table and gave them a watered-down version of our night-time visitation. I continued to savor my toast and waited for their reactions.

I also knew something was up. Kate had told me that they wanted me to help with Max's memorial and I could sense that they had a big plan. "One of you, spit it out."

Kate swallowed a mouthful of toast. What she said was stilted, like she had rehearsed a speech. That usually meant that she was sure I would nix the plan. *Double, double, toil and trouble,* I thought.

"We want Max's memorial to be a real tribute to him," she said. "We think that showcasing a few scenes from Macbeth will be the way to do that. His Aunt Mary told me that it was his favorite and that he was looking forward to performing for the Rhett Street Players." She pointed to the others. "Shelia would play Lady Macbeth, and Matt's role would be Macbeth. You would direct the scenes and I can handle the props. The set is finished and and the community is just waiting to see what you can do as a director. I'm sure Max would be pleased if we incorporated the play into his memorial. I know that supporters would give more money in Max's name for our cause." She pushed her plate away and looked at me. "Don't frown. You can do this." I stared back at her. Before I could say no, however, the doorbell rang again.

"Saved by the bell," I shouted.

Bill walked into the kitchen. This time he was wearing a coat and tie—his working uniform. "How's your ankle?" he asked.

I looked down at my foot. My ankle had turned into a ball with a small puce and dark yellow ink blot but it didn't hurt as much when I put my weight on it. "Much better," I said.

He motioned for me to follow him into the study. "Describe for me what happened last night."

I told him the little I knew and then he closed his notebook and got up to leave.

Everyone was talking at once as I entered the kitchen. "We must keep going," Kate said. "I want us to go up and look at the stage. The show must go on."

Shelia picked up her script and looked at each of us. "That sounds like we don't care. Should we really have a memorial for Max after all that has happened to Simmons and the mansion? What do you think, Simmons?"

I looked around at everybody. I could see the eagerness in Kate's eyes. I knew it was necessary to honor Max and continue to raise money for the Rhett Street Players. Could I justify putting Aunt Stacy and myself in possible danger by continuing to live here and work with the Rhett Street Players? Why would anyone want to harm me or the mansion?

Yet, someone had done that very thing last night. The scare was real. We'd discovered a tunnel and then everything had started happening. The quilt, a piece of McBee history that might get us recognized as a historical site had been stolen. Aunt Stacy came over and put her arm around me. She squeezed my shoulder and gave me an encouraging look. I looked down at my shirt. Would I shrivel or roar? I had never backed off from a challenge or a threat.

I thought of my mother fighting for the Women's Lib Movement. I could almost hear her voice telling me to "keep on keeping on." She would say that "life is like riding a bicycle. To keep your balance, you must keep moving." Later I learned she was quoting Albert Einstein.

I took a deep breath. "Let's get this show on the road." I said. "We don't have much time to put it together. Kate, I know you have a million notes, but we need to look at the stage and think about which scenes we want to do and get it organized."

Kate clapped her hands and everyone shouted a big hooray. "You have made the right choice," she said. "Let's finish up here and go upstairs."

Everyone pitched in and got the kitchen cleaned up. Aunt Stacy decided to stay with me for another night and went over to her condo to get clean clothes.

On the way upstairs, I decided to begin my directing. "I don't want any of you to forget that this is the Scottish Play that we are dealing with. Do NOT say the name of the play once we get up to the stage. I don't want to take any chances. We have had enough tragedy to last a lifetime."

Everyone nodded and, with a quiet reverence, we walked into the room and up to the stage.

It was the first time I had been on the third floor since the murder and there was an eerie feeling in the air. We sat down in the chairs and began to discuss the easiest scenes to do. Kate wanted us to do several, but I felt that two well-known scenes would be plenty. Our focus would be Max and what he had contributed to the world of theater.

While the rest of the group continued to debate the best scenes, I went up the steps to the stage and walked across to the prop table. A new dagger was wedged into the table and held a piece of blood-stained paper. I screamed and backed away.

Kate was the first to get to me. She looked at the table. "Don't touch it," she said.

Through tears, I read the note. "Foul is fair. If you don't back off, you better beware."

16

Several days passed after that and I didn't hear from Bill. The memory of his angry face was burned into my brain. He had taken the dagger and note and stomped down the steps. "We will get this cretin!" he yelled over his shoulder as he stormed out of the front door of the mansion.

Bill must care a lot, I thought. I smiled, but admitted to myself that I wasn't certain that I was ready for a serious relationship. He wasn't either if he hadn't been in touch.

Stacy and I made a point of checking off the to-do list for Max's memorial. At the end of our third long day of polishing silver, cleaning Uncle Hugh's crystal, and washing and drying the china, I decided to use the second best for company, if I ever had any—English Royal Doulton that served twelve. Truthfully, I hoped never to see that many people hungry at my house unless they wanted store-bought slaw and burgers on the grill.

It was a comfort to have Aunt Stacy to help. We sat out on the terrace at the end of every day with a glass of pinot grigio and I listened to the stories she remembered about her in-laws, the McBees. After a cleaning service had finished removing dust bunnies (and maybe even a few large dust hares) from the mansion, everything sparkled. Except me. I needed some time to get my head on straight. Too much had happened and I couldn't sort it.

The tunnel had been closed. The dumbwaiter could no longer be used. I had changed the locks and added dead bolts, but I still didn't feel safe. I had been violated.

My cell phone buzzed. It was Kate. "I'm going over to the costume shop in Greenville. Want to come?"

"Just what I need to clear the cobwebs from my head. Aunt Stacy and I have McBee ready for the memorial."

"We need to go into rehearsals right away. Be there soon."

Aunt Stacy had planned to go back to the Rosemont Library to do more research in the archives and history section in the South Carolina Room. She was determined that McBee Mansion would end up with a plaque on the door.

I rushed upstairs and threw on an Aly Daly dress and my favorite Espadrilles. I was standing on the stoop when Kate drove up.

We took the interstate and ended up at the costume shop in less than twenty minutes. On the way, Kate told me that a lot of people from New York wanted to come in order to honor Max so it would be prudent to have a lot of rehearsals for the Macbeth scenes and several more board meetings so everyone would be on the same page. I wasn't sure that the board would be on the same page ever, but we had announced that the memorial would be on Saturday the 15th of September. There was plenty of time.

The Old Curios and Costumes Emporium sat on a hill across the street from a plumbing company and around the corner from the Wade Meyers Highway. I remembered this place from years before when I did Children's Theater at the Theater on the Green. The musty smell of old clothes hit me in the face as we walked into an open hallway—the same smell that sometimes haunts small community theaters.

A jolly older man came out of the shadows. "May I help you? I'm Andrew." He dusted off his pants and adjusted the tie on his starched white shirt. A gold watch chain hung from his vest pocket. He looked like he had stepped off the stage of a serious production of Dorian Gray.

I looked at Kate and motioned for her to take the lead. After she explained that we were looking for authentic Macbeth costumes, he led us into a room that looked like a Shakespearian set. Mannequins were dressed in dark and heavy velvet robes. There was also a mixture of royal costumes.

My eyes were drawn to the exact robe that would be perfect for a Macbeth character. Kate had already snatched up a royal gown for Shelia—it was perfect for Lady Macbeth.

"We want to reserve these," Kate said. "Do you alter if it is needed?"

"Of course," Andrew replied. "I can hold these for you. When will the cast be in to try them on?"

"Shelia and Matt can come over on Saturday. Will that be okay?"

"Will the other actors be coming in, too?" Andrew asked.

Kate shook her head. "There are only two actors. We are doing just a couple of scenes for a memorial for Max Everhart."

"Oh," he said. "That's odd. A man was in looking at costumes for Macbeth just the other day."

Kate shrugged. "I have a poster announcing Max's memorial in my car. Would you put it in your window for us?"

"Yes. I'll be happy to put it up for you and I hope I can attend. I saw Max's last play when I was in New York. It was smashing."

We put a deposit down. While Andrew ran the card, I asked him about the man he had mentioned looking for MacBeth costumes.

"Well," he said, "he was an older gentleman. Maybe in his sixties…well dressed. He had a mustache and walked with a cane. He didn't rent anything. I figured he was a high school drama teacher thinking about what to do next term. I get a lot of those."

My cell phone rang and I stepped away from the counter. It was Bill. I told him that Kate and I were soon on our way back from Greenville.

"I'm in Greenville, too—leaving the sheriff's department. Why don't you meet me at North Hampton Wines. I'm craving one of their Black Angus burgers."

"Sure." Kate and I both loved their charcuterie board with a crisp Chateau Miraval rosé.

We got there first. When Bill arrived, we were seated by a window that looked across a downtown street to condos that were fairly new. "Aunt Stacy is a walking history book about the city of Greenville," I told Kate. "She says that where the condos are used to be the trolley barn." She had even claimed that her great Uncle Taylor had a store where a Publix now sat. I would have been more interested if the trolley barn had been an opera house.

Bill ordered a scotch and water. At a meeting with the sheriff, he had been advised that there were no fingerprints on the original dagger that killed Max. All of the blood on the scene had been Max's. It seemed that the killer had planned the murder because it was carefully executed. It was clear—someone had wanted Max dead.

Kate sipped her rosé. "What would the motive be?"

Bill thought for a moment. "There is always greed. Then there is revenge…passion…jealousy. I personally think that if I find a money trail, I will find my killer. That is the short answer."

I sighed. "I don't want to hear the long answer. It seems as if this will never end. I'm ready to sit down in the study at McBee, write a play and get on with my life. But until we get all of this settled, I don't feel like I can do a good job for the Theater."

Bill took a bite of his burger and drank some iced tea. "Jackson saw someone the other day that wants to look at the mansion. I told him that I wasn't sure it was still on the market. One of his investors is bringing their company to Rosemont and since he is the CEO, he is looking for a show house for entertaining."

"Tell Jackson to talk to Eric. I have been having a great time cleaning and making the place look like the mansion that it is. Maybe Eric will have another place to show him."

Kate and Bill looked at each other and grinned. "I know that it has been a hard decision," said Kate, "but we are happy that you want to keep the mansion in the family."

I smiled and nodded. "Aunt Stacy has been telling me funny stories about the McBees and the historical significance of the place. Did you know that Uncle Thomas McBee stood on the stoop at the end of WWI and read all the names of the soldiers from Rosemont that were killed? We may also find a major connection to the Civil War. It could be turned into a museum." I paused and made a sad face. "Or I could live there and pay a fortune just to turn the heat on this winter."

"Or you could live there and rent the top floor to the Rhett Street Players," Kate said.

All done himself, Bill watched as we finished our dinner. "You don't need to make a decision right away. If you closed the vents in some of the rooms, the A/C wouldn't cost as much." He pushed back in his chair. "Simmons, I have a few leads from the case that I can't share, but rest assured I am going to apprehend Max's killer. I am still certain that Veronica was killed by the same person."

"Do you have *anything* you can share?" I said. Kate and I looked at him expectantly and he grinned. "Buy my dessert and I will spill the beans."

"You're on. Chai Spiced Cheesecake or the Mousse Au Chocolat?"

We ordered the mousse to share. I took a bite and almost swooned. Bill and Kate enjoyed the rest of it and then Bill began to fill us in on the investigation.

"What I'm about to tell you will be online in the *Greenville News* tomorrow—a recap of our progress. I interviewed a person of interest a few days ago. This person saw Max get out of his car and go into the back door of the mansion. She had come over to the mansion to put a centerpiece on the table before the board meeting. She was going to speak to him, but she had to go home and walk her poodle before the board meeting started. She didn't see or hear anyone else but could confirm the time."

"That must have been Maddie Taylor," Kate said. "She was in charge of setting up."

I shook my head. "Matt and Shelia were there. Weren't they? I am confused about the timeline. Did they leave and come back? Why didn't they hear anything or see anything if they were down on the second floor painting the background for the set? Had they left before the meeting started?"

I had lots of questions and Bill still wasn't forthcoming with some of the answers. "Do you think that the murder and the attack on the mansion are related? Is the killer trying to scare me and Aunt Stacy?"

"I don't think Maddie did it," Kate answered. "She told me that she wanted you for a neighbor. She doesn't want you to sell the place."

"I can confirm that," Bill said, "but there may be something else we don't know."

"This is becoming a tangled web." My iPhone buzzed in my summer straw bag. Saint Francis Hospital. My hand shook as I listened to the message.

"It's Aunt Stacy," I told Kate and Bill. "She was coming out of the Rosemont Library and someone pushed her down the steps. She's at Saint Francis."

"Come on," said Bill. "Leave your car here. I'll throw the blue light on top of my car and we will be there in a few minutes."

Kate waved as we left the parking lot. As we sped through several red lights, fear gripped my stomach and I wiped tears from my cheeks. My imagination was going wild. Aunt Stacy was my only living relative.

17

In spite of Aunt Stacy's protests, the doctor kept her overnight for observation. I tossed and turned for most of the night until Maxie finally jumped off the bed. The alarm went off and when I got up, Maxie was sitting on the windowsill. A cardinal was jumping through the branches of the water oak by my bedroom window.

"Don't even think of a redbird for breakfast," I said. "I will give you your favorite cat food with a sprinkle of tuna on top. Follow me to the kitchen." Maxie came right behind me as if she understood. I wondered if I could put a collar and a leash on her. "Would you like to walk outside with me?" She gave me a resounding meow.

The sun was coming up as I walked into the kitchen. After two cups of coffee and a green smoothie, I phoned the hospital. Aunt Stacy was chomping at the bit. "Come get me at once," she hollered. "This place is noisy and full of people."

"I will get clean clothes for you and be there soon," I said. I was gathering up Aunt Stacy's toiletries and clothes when Joan called.

"I miss you," she said," and started to sob. Through hiccups, more sobs, and large gulps of air, she tried to explain that she and Jim had broken up and she knew it was her fault because she always complained that he worked too much. They'd been going to Soby's for an early dinner and the Peace Center for a new show when he'd gotten a call about a horse in labor in Travelers Rest. Before they sat down to eat, he'd left and called an Uber for her.

"Ride with me to pick up Aunt Stacy at the hospital," I said. "I'll explain everything when I get there. I'll pick you up in a few minutes."

Joan was standing outside when I pulled up. I unlocked the car and she jumped in. I explained about Aunt Stacy's falling down the library steps, and then, to distract Joan from her breakup with Jim, I started recounting everything that had happened since I moved from New York.

It felt good to unload and put all the events into perspective. Unloading didn't help to figure out what to do about it, but I felt a lot lighter in my mind and more focused on how Aunt Stacy and I could handle it. "One day at a time" seemed to run through my mind.

Joan and I agreed that the tunnel and whatever had been there were not likely connected to the murders. I couldn't decide if the killer was after me because of information I had and didn't know I had. Had I done something to inflame the situation? I took a deep breath and tried not to imagine what could happen next. *Present fears are less than horrible imaginings.*

Joan started telling me about her problems with Jim. "I told him he needed to hire a partner to help with his vet practice. He told me I needed to hire an assistant to help run the Inn. Neither of us wants to really do that. If we could both get away, we could talk it through."

"I agree," I said. "Compromise is in order for both of you if you want to have a relationship. You both have demanding jobs. Think about that," I said. Joan sniffed, blew her nose and nodded.

Aunt Stacy was waiting at the hospital entrance in a wheelchair holding a bunch of papers in her lap. "It's about time you got here," she said as we got out of the car. "We have to go by the pharmacy. I have to take a prescribed analgesic. Joan, you put the wheelchair inside. Simmons, get me settled in the Volvo."

I smiled. Aunt Stacy was her bossy self. I felt better already. The Greenville Discount Pharmacy was close to the hospital and only took a few minutes to get there. This was the preferred pharmacy for most of the families within miles. I left the car running and popped into the store. As usual, Mike was behind the counter. Eric Loftis was standing at the counter with a package in his hand. He quickly closed the top of the bag and turned to me.

"Boy am I am glad to see you. You've never signed the first copy of the contract to sell McBee Mansion. No problem, though—I have a revised version. I've been out of town and haven't had a chance to see you. I can't really entertain offers if I don't have a contract."

I handed Aunt Stacy's prescription to Mike and turned to face Eric. "As I've already told you, I'm not ready to sign a contract. I'm not sure anymore that I want to sell. I know that you have had some buyers that wanted to look, but since then, we have closed off the tunnel, changed the locks, and made it a safer place to live. So I'm thinking of staying."

Eric shook his head in frustration. "First, when you called from New York, you couldn't wait to sell it. Now, you may not want to sell it at all. Simmons, make up your mind. As soon as the memorial service is over, we need to get on the same page." He turned and strode out of the store. Mike handed me Aunt Stacy's medication, pretending he hadn't heard the exchange. I paid and thanked him.

18

"Too many cooks have spoiled the broth," Aunt Stacy said. She put her crossword puzzle on the side table and looked over at me.

I closed the cookbook that I was reading. *The Blue Zones Kitchen* was fascinating. I wanted to live to be 100, but Aunt Stacy looked healthy enough to outlive us all. She had recovered faster than I had—I still felt twinges in my ankle. "You don't have to worry about cooking tonight," I said. "Joan is bringing food and I have wine. She is lonely since she and Jim have broken up."

"I didn't mean food. I meant too many suspects and no one guilty. I know that you and Kate have gone over the list a million times. I think we have missed something, and Bill isn't sharing any information. Let's start at the beginning," Aunt Stacy said.

I looked out the window of the study. It would soon be fall with cooler nights and amazing low humidity days. Max's memorial was in two weeks and we had one more board meeting to finalize the plans. The weather would be perfect.

"The beginning of all of this would be that first board meeting," I said. "The day Max was killed. Since he was stabbed in the back, I suppose even an older woman could have done it. We need to think about where everyone was when the lights went out."

"How do you know that he was killed when the lights went out?" Aunt Stacy asked.

I thought for a moment. "You know, I don't." Another question floated into my mind. "Did Matt and Shelia leave before Max arrived? We only have their word for where they were and what they were doing. In fact, that's true with everybody in the house at the time."

Aunt Stacy nodded. "There could have been someone here that we don't even know about. The killer could have hidden in one of the rooms that we never use and waited for the right time to attack Max. Isn't that true?"

"That could mean that we will never know who his killer was." I looked out the window again. "I still believe that the same person killed Veronica. Don't you?" I asked. "Nothing else makes sense."

Aunt Stacy picked up her puzzle and nodded.

I couldn't go back to my book. I grabbed my hobo bag that was hanging on the coat rack. "I'm going to take a walk to clear my head," I called to Aunt Stacy, and slipped out of the side door of the study.

Maybe the beginning *wasn't* at the first board meeting. My mind was spinning as I walked through the backyard gate and followed the path of the collapsed tunnel beneath my feet. The tunnel was now hidden under massive layers of dirt—only someone who knew it was there would have been able to use it to get in and out of the mansion. Did everyone on the board know about the hidden tunnel?

I strolled along for an undetermined amount of time and looked up to find I had walked all the way to Main Street. A cool breeze blew through the alley behind the Savory Corner.

I opened the door to the shop and chilled air assaulted my face like a glass of ice water gurgling in a parched throat. Late August in the South meant below-zero temperatures in stores and shops.

Aromas that made my stomach rumble wafted through the air. I ordered a blueberry scone and a frothy cappuccino and sat down. As I sipped my drink, I thought about all the history connected with the mansion—from raids by native Americans to a possible connection to the Underground Railroad to a probable Prohibition-era speakeasy. I also hadn't forgotten the death of Alfred Redfern, but the family always said that he missed a step and rolled down the full three flights of the front hallway steps and broke his neck. I could never get any of my relatives to tell the whole story, but I think he was attending the weekly poker game at the mansion and I was sure that liquor was involved. Maybe even bathtub gin.

I kept running suspects through my brain. Eric really wanted to sell the mansion, so I couldn't imagine him doing damage to it. Sally Goldman might want the work that she would get from promoting Max and the theater—so she would not kill the golden goose. I read once in a D.C. Smith novel that all crimes are caused by selfishness. Hmmm. Who was the most selfish one on the board?

Maddie, Myrtle and even Margaret Sellars had their own agendas. Maddie would have known about the tunnel since she'd grown up across the street. As a child, she could have played in the tunnels—and on the dumbwaiter. The agendas of ladies of Rosemont's polite society didn't likely include scare tactics—or murder.

Even if Shelia and Matt were lying, they didn't fit into the timeline for the murder. Max was killed right before or right after the lights went out—and they were already gone.

I couldn't prove any of this, so I had to trust Bill to find the killer. But, as Aunt Stacy would say, I was like a dog chewing on a bone. I couldn't let it go—she and I had become risks to the actual killer and could be sitting ducks for another murder. Or, the incidents that had happened could simply be scare tactics meant to get us out of the mansion. Either way, it was all unsettling and there was no doubt that Aunt Stacy and I were in some sort of danger. I could have been in the study when the pipe bomb blew up the tunnel.

I thought of Woody Allen's quote from his book *Without Feathers. It's not that I'm afraid to die. I just don't want to be there when it happens.*

I finished my scone and decided to walk on down to the edge of the river. I couldn't get rid of a nagging feeling that I knew something important but it wouldn't rise to the surface of my brain. After I searched my memory a few times, I looked up and realized that I was on the bank of the Reedy River.

Max *must* have done something to provoke the killer. Money could be a motive, but not that I knew of for any of the people on the board. Unless Jackson doesn't have the money Kate thinks he had—the Taylors thought he had made bad investments in his old job. But that wouldn't have anything to do with Max.

Kate still held on to the theory that a disgruntled actor from New York had confronted Max in a fit of rage. Maybe the killer hadn't meant to kill Max, but when he picked up the dagger, Max had turned away from him and the killer just stabbed him and ran. Maybe even ran through the tunnel. But that wasn't a plausible theory—an actor from New York wouldn't have known about the tunnel. I was pretty sure Max hadn't known anything about it either.

My phone buzzed with a text from Joan. "Running late, new guests arriving late. Hope to be there by seven but may have to take a raincheck."

I put the phone back in my pocket and trudged up the hill. I knew I needed to start running again but it was too hot in Rosemont in August to run outside. I would look into joining the YMCA.

By the time I got back to the mansion, Aunt Stacy was in the kitchen finishing up snacks to go with our wine. I told her that Joan might not make it to dinner. The sun was going down, so we sat on the patio on the south side of the mansion.

The view of Farris Hill stretched out in the distance. I sipped my rosé and thought about how lucky I was to live in town. "I can't sell a view like this," I said. "If only I could afford to keep this place up. Kate has offered for the Theater Board to pay me for rehearsal space, but I'm not sure that would be enough. I want to write plays and work for the Rhett Street Players. It doesn't look like that will be a possibility."

I looked at Aunt Stacy and saw a huge grin on her face. "It could be if you are interested in *my* proposal," she said.

"What proposal?"

"Eric has agreed to sell my condo in the Woodlands."

"Where would you live if you sell your condo?"

"Here, of course. Think about it. Since I've been staying here, we have only seen each other for meals and late afternoon chats. I would pay my share of the budget to keep this old girl running and live in the east wing of the second floor. I could have a bedroom, bath, den and the extra room for my arts and crafts. That's bigger than my condo.

Best of all, I could keep working on getting us on the Historical Register. We could keep up the house, preserve McBee's historical heritage *and* live in the center of town."

I stood up from my chair, looked across at the glorious sunset view and gave Aunt Stacy a hug. "You are a genius. We can make this work. We *will* stay here and not let a developer turn our mansion into a bunch of high-rise condos."

She smiled. "Come up to that wing of the mansion. I'll show you what could be my sanctuary and how it could be renovated without harming the historical value of the house."

Maxie was asleep on the sofa, and I left her to her afternoon cat nap. I followed Aunt Stacy up the stairs and into her suite. She grabbed her journal and we sat on the bed and looked at her drawings. She only wanted to knock out a wall between her bedroom and the suite next to hers. This would give her the extra rooms to make an apartment for herself.

There were a few possible barriers to her plans. For one, we might have to make sure with the Historic Register that a slight renovation would be okay, but if a future owner wanted to put the wall back, it wouldn't be hard.

Aunt Stacy tapped the page of her journal. "First, we need to get a contractor to see if this is a load-bearing wall. We'd need three estimates, I think."

I jumped up and down like a silly schoolgirl and threw my arms around her. We could save the mansion, save money, *and* save ourselves. This was the perfect solution!

Aunt Stacy and I poured over the drawings some more. We were absorbed in the future of our home, each making suggestions. I thought I heard the door, but when no one called out, we continued talking about the future and how long it would take to get all the permits and get started. I knew Aunt Stacy would first have to close on her place in the Woodlands.

It would be fun to have this project for the winter. With the right contractor and work crew we could have Aunt Stacy settled by next spring. Aunt Stacy closed her journal and smiled. I hugged her again.

Just then, a huge meow echoed through the mansion like a hungry mountain cat after its prey. Maxie was far too small to make that much noise, I thought, but empty rooms echoed and bounced the sound against the walls. I jumped up and headed for the stairs.

By the time I reached the study, Maxie had stopped yowling. She sat on the floor batting around what looked like a tangle of threads. "I wonder where this came from," I said. "You really *are* more dog than cat. You're even a watchdog!" Grandmother always said that every crow thinks theirs is the blackest. I understood what that old adage meant. Maxie was the smartest cat I had ever seen.

19

The following morning slipped by. I had tossed and turned all night until Maxie had finally jumped off the bed and slept in her cat bed. I was running on coffee fumes, but neither Aunt Stacy nor I wanted lunch—we sat across from each other and tried to enjoy the leftovers from food Joan had brought a couple of nights before. I took a bite of the black-eyed pea salad. The chef at the Inn always added mint and onions with a sprig of dill on top. It was one of my favorites and yet I was too upset to eat.

My iPhone was on the table by my plate and I jumped when it played "By the Seaside." Aunt Stacy grabbed it and answered it for me. She mumbled a few words and hung up.

"Grab your purse," she said. "That was Bob Matthews. He is working at Rock House Antiques this afternoon. We've got to get over there. Some old man dropped the quilt off and asked the Rock House to do an appraisal. Bob recognized the quilt—he was at the Historical Society meeting when I presented the quilt as proof of McBee Mansion being a part of the Underground Railroad."

I followed Aunt Stacy out the door, fumbling for my new door key. I finally locked the door and we jumped into the Volvo.

Bob Matthews had always been at the Rock House. Mother would make me come with her when I was a little girl. She never bought anything but always said that she got inspiration. We would spend a morning looking at the different booths and what they had to offer. When we got home, she would call Zero, our yardman—a nickname because that was about what he actually did. Instead, he would come over and spend the rest of the day moving furniture and lamps to different rooms in our house.

By the time Daddy got home, the house would have a totally different look. He once said that he always had to look before he sat in his den chair because it moved more than he did. Mother would just laugh and pick up a book.

When we pulled in, a patrol car and Bill's car were parked in front of the shop. Aunt Stacy jumped out and raced in before I could even turn the ignition off.

I took a deep breath. I hadn't seen Bill in quite a while. I shook off the thought, plastered a smile on my lips, and walked into a hornet's nest. Aunt Stacy had both hands on one side of the quilt's frame. Bill was holding on to the other side.

"Do *not* even think of trying to take our quilt." Aunt Stacy's voice was several octaves above normal. "We have to get this authenticated. The Ledbetters from the Historical Society are waiting for proof that this very quilt was used as a symbol of the Underground Railroad. They say that if a wagon-wheel-patterned quilt was hanging by the stoop or on a clothesline, it was safe for the runaways to come in. I know for a fact that this quilt was often hung on the clothesline."

Aunt Stacy let her arms drop from the frame and glared at Bill with a "I dare you to dispute me" look. I put my hand on her shoulder.

I knew that Bill needed to take the quilt as evidence. "Who brought the quilt into the shop?"

Bill nodded in appreciation. "Let's start at the beginning. Bob, can you describe the person that brought in the quilt? Then we can work out a compromise about when the family can have the quilt back."

I gave him a short version of my best stink eye and he almost smiled. Aunt Stacy snarled. She and I would fight them for possession of the quilt, and they knew it.

Bob rubbed his hand over his bald head. "He was elderly and had a mustache. And I think he had a cane." He looked up, trying to remember. "The painterly ladies were here. They were hanging work for their art show next week." He paused again. "It was a mad house that day. The man said that he wanted an appraisal and would be back by later to pick it up, so I grabbed an intake voucher. When I turned back around to ask his name, he was gone."

I couldn't help thinking that our quilt thief matched a description of the man asking about Macbeth robes at the costume shop in Greenville. I had mentioned it to Bill when he'd met Kate and me for lunch afterward.

Bill turned back to Bob. "Did you see what car he was driving?"

"I didn't see a car. But I called the police and them right away." He gestured at Aunt Stacy and me. "Simmons had told me that Aunt Stacy would bring the quilt in later this week and the old man seemed suspicious."

"What do you mean?" asked Bill.

"Now that I think of it, he had on brown leather gloves. It must be a hundred and one under that water oak out there. Who wears brown leather gloves in late summer in Rosemont?"

"Did he take the gloves off?" Bill asked. "Could his hands have given him away if he had on a costume and wasn't an old man at all?"

"It could have been Max's killer, but why would he steal the quilt?" Aunt Stacy said.

"If he needed money," I said out loud.

Everyone looked at me and I shrugged my shoulders. Money was always mentioned as a motive for murder and I knew the quilt had to be valuable.

"Well, at least it looks none the worse for wear," Aunt Stacy said. "Give me a hand with the other side, Simmons. It will fit in the back of the Volvo if we put the seats down."

Bill stepped in front of Aunt Stacy and shook his head. "Not only is it evidence, but if it is as valuable as you think it is, it will be safer at the police station. If you take it back to McBee Mansion and hang it over the study mantel, the thief could try to steal it again. You and Simmons will have to come to the station and be fingerprinted. Would you be able to come this afternoon?"

"Fingerprinted?" Aunt Stacy whispered. "We didn't steal the quilt. Well, I never! I have never been this embarrassed. How dare you even consider this, Bill Randolph! Your Aunt Sissy will hear about this. Accusing me and Simmons."

Bill tried to keep the smile off his face. "Ms. McBee, the person that stole the quilt may have left fingerprints on it. By eliminating the fingerprints we know, we may be able to find out the truth. Do you want to follow me now?"

It was close to five by the time we finished with the police. Bill told me that he would call later.

My hands were covered in ink and Aunt Stacy said that she looked like the wreck of the Hesperus. I kept forgetting to look up that expression. I knew it was probably something Aunt Stacy had learned in English class. We pulled in behind the house and saw half the Rhett Street Board in the yard. Myrtle was directing the action. It was more chaotic than a stage set. Margaret had bright red readers slipping down her nose from the "glistening" on her face. She was scribbling into a notebook and Maddie was placing stones on the ground where Myrtle would point.

Aunt Stacy tapped me on the shoulder. "Those women looked bedraggled. Let's invite them in for a cold drink."

I climbed the front steps and turned around. "Come in for some iced tea and cool off," I said. All three women almost knocked me over trying to get to the door before I did. The air conditioner was pumping out cold air. We sat at the table and Aunt Stacy filled a plate with brownies Joan had dropped by.

Aunt Stacy told about the fingerprinting process and then Maddie went off on how to decorate the tables for the wine and beer. Margaret wanted to use hydrangeas as the only flowers for decorations. Myrtle was interrupting all of us with thoughts of her own. I had no idea how we could pull off this memorial for Max.

I heard footsteps coming from the front hall steps and Matt appeared in the kitchen. Shelia was right behind him.

"Thanks for the key," he said. "Shelia and I had a great rehearsal. Your ideas were perfect for the setting. I hope you can be with us tomorrow. We have a few questions about how dark and damp the scene should be. I know it reflects the character of Macbeth, but doesn't it also show the secrecy and deception?"

"I will be back on track tomorrow," I said. "Aunt Stacy and I had too many distractions today."

All three women started talking at once. "We were all finger-printed a few days ago. Do you think Detective Randolph is close to finding the killer? I'm sure he has eliminated all of us by now."

I let my mind wander while they continued to chatter. It was obvious that Bill wanted to compare prints that he may have taken off the dagger with the prints on the frame of the quilt, but he couldn't do that—the old man who'd stolen the quilt was wearing gloves when he took it to The Rock House.

Was one person responsible for all these crimes? What if he had an accomplice? Could there be two different people? What if more than one board member was involved?

Why did I continue to think that a board member was involved? The murder had occurred, either right before or during the blackout. My gut feeling led me to believe this.

Aunt Stacy put her hand on mine and smiled. "Simmons, earth calling."

I looked across the table. Maddie and Margaret were looking at the design for the tables. Shelia and Matt were hunched over them. Myrtle sat with her hands folded in her lap. "Yes, we all agree," she said. "This is how the garden should look. As soon as we know how many people are coming to the memorial, we can order the tables."

"Should we have chairs?" Margaret asked.

My iPhone vibrated in my pocket. A sneak peek told me that it was Bill. I left the table and went into the hall.

"I need to come over after work," he said. "Will you and Aunt Stacy be there?"

"Of course, but what's this about?" I asked.

"We can talk when I get there. I'll see you around seven. I'll bring dinner." He hung up.

If he is bringing dinner, maybe it's a social call. Then again, he could be bringing bad news and wants to soften the blow.

I shook my head. There couldn't be any bad news. We had had enough bad news to last a lifetime. I tried to recall the lines from Macbeth about good news but I couldn't come up with them. My mind was on overload.

20

"Grand Central Station!" Aunt Stacy yelled as she opened the door. Kate and Jackson joined Eric, who was sitting at the desk in the study. Jim had talked to Bill earlier in the day and he'd agreed that everyone should be there, and word had traveled faster than the ball in Times Square drops on New Year's Eve. It felt great to have the support of all these friends.

The doorbell chimed yet again. Had Bill invited everyone to the house? I had been under the impression he just wanted to talk to me and Aunt Stacy. Was he going to announce the killer? Probably not. Agatha Christie wasn't his style.

Joan and Jim, an item again, had come over earlier, and the mystery of why she'd not made our nightly dinners was solved. She had told me they'd both promised to try harder to see more of each other. If Jim got a call on a date night, Joan would go with him. I wondered what would happen if Joan had a late check-in and Jim had a horse with colic at the same time. I would sit back and watch the results of their new plan. It was worth the entertainment—I didn't have a plan for date nights with anyone.

133

Bill came in with a stack of pizzas and handed pictures of the quilt he had taken at the station to Aunt Stacy. He'd found out that the Historical Society would accept pictures of an item if they were accompanied by a notarized letter that the object had always been in the family.

I had planned to spend part of the afternoon going over a contract for Aunt Stacy's condo—Eric said he already had a potential buyer and she could move her furniture as soon as she signed the contract. Most of her furniture was antique and would fit better in the mansion. They dwarfed the low ceilings of her condo anyway.

Kate had already started planning where each piece should go in the suite upstairs. We had decided that Aunt Stacy should go ahead and move, live in the space for a while, and we would remodel after Christmas.

Eric finished signing his part of the contract and put his pen in the pocket inside his sport coat. It was a Montblanc! My mind flashed back to the day Aunt Stacy and I were in the tunnel—*that* pen had been a Montblanc too.

Bill cleared his throat and everyone got quiet.

"EF Hutton must be somewhere around here," said Aunt Stacy. Everyone looked at her like she had three heads. She made a face. "That was an ad on TV years ago. When EF Hutton spoke, everyone listened. All of you are too young to remember my kind of TV." She looked around the room at the still blank faces. "Anyway, we are all ears for Bill's report."

Bill cleared his throat again and looked straight at me. "I'm happy to hear that Aunt Stacy will be living here, but it would still be better for both of you to move out until we have totally resolved the case. Chief Madison has decided to dig out the tunnel and find out if there is anything of value that would lead us to the killer… but I have already told you too much." He glanced around the table. "Can any of you convince Simmons that it isn't safe here?"

The proverbial pin could have dropped. Nobody said a word.

Bill looked at me again. "I can *make* you go if I have to."

Wait, I thought. He had gathered everyone for dinner so other people could convince us to leave temporarily? It's a crime scene and he's the detective. He should be able to just get on with it and leave us alone.

"I'm staying," I said.

Aunt Stacy chimed in. "Me too."

Bill nodded his head. "I fully expected that response. And I don't want to force you to go. So our department will work out a way to keep security here 24/7." Bill gathered his notes and stood up to leave. Jim and Aunt Stacy insisted that he stay.

Just then, the doorbell rang and the fresh aroma of pepperoni pizza floated from the front hall into the dining room—more pizza had arrived. Joan had put paper plates, paper napkins, and plastic forks on the antique table. Aunt Stacy rolled her eyes and sat down with the rest of us.

I grinned at her. "I know you hate paper and plastic, but you need to be thankful that we are sitting at the table and not passing a box while we sit on the floor in the sun room." Everybody laughed.

After we each had a large slice of pizza in front of us, Jim glanced over at me. "How is that calico you rescued from the bushes?"

Before I could answer, Eric jumped into the conversation. "It's a good thing that beast has nine lives. I have never liked cats—and that cat doesn't like me. Give me a good ole black lab, any day."

"Don't worry, Eric," I said. "She's asleep on my bed. Besides, Maxie is more like a dog than a cat. She's even a watch cat." I looked at Jim. "Do you think it would be possible for me to train Maxie to a leash? She follows me around all the time." Bill tried to squelch a chuckle.

Kate looked knowingly at me. "I suppose that you and I will have to walk Maxie through the neighborhood on a leash. We can get her a collar and leash to match our outfits."

The entire group burst out in gales of laughter. Even Eric thought that was funny so I decided that, if Maxie agreed, she and Eric might possibly become friends.

The table topic shifted to the memorial. Kate, Joan and I discussed what we were planning to wear and Kate and I decided to go shopping in Greenville the next day.

The party finally broke up about 9:30 and people drifted out. On his way out, Eric promised to schedule a test visit with Maxie, and I promised that she would be on her best behavior.

Bill was the last to leave. He lingered near the front door. I looked in his eyes and thought that my soul could get lost in those liquid chocolate pools. He placed his hands on my shoulder and I could feel the heat from his body.

I could tell what he was about to say was serious, but the door banged open and Eric came charging back in. "I left part of my contract copy on the table," he said, shaking his head. "This is the third time this week I have lost either a pen or some important papers. I even left my jacket at the office yesterday." He darted into the dining room and rushed back out the door.

Bill waved good night to me too. Our moment had passed.

I locked the front door and started for the stairs when Aunt Stacy called to me from the kitchen. She was looking at the contract Eric had left behind. "I don't understand part of this contract. Will you come look at it?"

It had been a long day, but Aunt Stacy rarely asked for my advice, so I turned around. I sat next to her at the kitchen table and realized immediately that the contract wasn't the same. Eric had added clauses that weren't normal for selling a condo. The language was vague and the earnest money seemed too high. Had Eric even read this document?

"One of his assistants must have done this for him," I told Aunt Stacy. "I will talk to him tomorrow. Don't sign anything until we have a clear picture of what your contract obligations are. It should not be this complicated. Once we have answers, I will call Gray Movers and see how soon we can get your furniture here."

I walked around turning off lights and Aunt Stacy climbed the front hall steps. I heard her phone ring and then she stopped and came back down to the study. "That was Maddie. She was walking her pug and saw someone run from the bushes to the backyard. She has called the police. Let's sit here until we see a police car drive up."

I took a deep breath and sat down next to Aunt Stacy in the dark room. She reached for my hand and quiet settled around us. Before I could take another breath, the incessant beating of our brass door knocker made me jump and almost fall off the sofa. "Open up!" a familiar voice shouted.

I cracked open the door. Matt stood there with a sheepish grin on his face. "I'm sorry. I left my playbook on the stage. I need to get it so I can practice my lines. I saw a light on in the kitchen and assumed you were still awake."

Bill's Ford screeched into the driveway. He jumped out, charged up the steps, and grabbed Matt's collar. "What were you doing in the bushes? Did you come back for the money?" Bill jerked Matt around and started pushing him down the front steps.

"Stop!" I said. "Matt wasn't hiding in the bushes. He came over to get his playbook. Do you think something is buried in the tunnel?"

Matt was bewildered. "I-I don't know anything about a tunnel. I parked in the back driveway and came around the front because I thought Simmons was still awake. I have to memorize more lines before Shelia and I rehearse tomorrow." He pointed across the street. "A lady from that house was walking her little dog and waved me down. She asked me if I had seen an old man coming out of the bushes, but she smelled like bourbon and I thought she was seeing things. I swear I'm telling the truth. If you don't believe me, go talk to her."

Bill looked at me and let go of Matt's arm, turned, and trotted across the street. I opened the door and motioned for Matt to come in. Aunt Stacy was beside me. "This is all too much for me," she said. "I'm going on to bed. We'll talk in the morning."

Matt hurried back with a notebook. "See you tomorrow," he said, waving as he disappeared around the corner of the house.

My head was spinning. "All the world's a stage" kept rolling through my mind. Was someone dressing up and playing a part to distract us from what was going on? Could the "old man" be Mr. Ledbetter from the Historical Society? Was Matt lying to us? Could the killer be a board member? Were the tunnel and the murder connected?

"Double, double toil and trouble." Bill had returned and was standing in front of me with a quizzical expression on his face and I realized I had said it out loud. He looked tired and hungry, so I gestured toward the kitchen. "Join me for scrambled eggs frittata?"

He looked at his watch. "It's 10:30 and I just got off from work. I would be happy to have a midnight snack with you." I got a big bowl out of the cabinet. I turned on Amazon music through Alexa and music from our high school days played softly in the background. I felt like we belonged in the kitchen at that very moment.

Bill opened the fridge and grabbed eggs, cherry tomatoes, zucchini, and mozzarella. I pinched basil from the plant in the window over the sink. The sky was clear and I could see stars as I mixed the ingredients together. Bill stood by the stove and leaned down to pick up Maxie. She had smelled the food and wandered in to see what was happening at this time of night. "She really likes you, you know," I said. "And she is picky about people. She tries to attack Eric. I found her the other day with a scrap of thread in her mouth. I wasn't joking when I said that she acts more like a watch dog. She totally ignores the fact that she isn't as big as Maddie's pug." I patted her on top of her head. She squeezed her eyes shut and meowed softly.

I brought out the Spode Italian dinner plates, put the Candlelight silver flatware beside them, and grabbed the navy linen dinner napkins. Bill sat opposite me at the kitchen table, Maxie curled up in his lap.

We finished the meal in silence, and I finally spoke again. "There have to be clues that I've missed, Bill. I just can't figure out why Max or Veronica would be killed for money," I said. "Is it possible that our thief and killer are the same? Or are there two people?"

Bill's phone buzzed and he looked at it. "I'm sorry, but I've got to go," he said. Before he left, though, he came around the table and kissed me softly on the forehead.

For the first time in weeks, I slept soundly through the night.

21

I had gone over to the Fresh Market to pick up a few last minute items before the board meeting. I pulled the Volvo around to the back of the mansion. Today's meeting was different from the first I'd attended. The mansion was home for me now.

Aunt Stacy was in the kitchen mixing up a fresh batch of sweet iced tea. I poured myself a glass and started slicing lemons. Myrtle had placed a bunch of hydrangeas in the center of the table. Maddie had brought over peach pound cake and fresh whipped cream.

There was nothing artificial about these Southern ladies—they could be as sweet as my Aunt Stacy's iced tea or as mean as a momma lion protecting her cubs. And yet I still couldn't imagine any of them stabbing Max Everhart or drowning Veronica.

Other board members trickled into the dining room. Joan sat across from me and, after a few minutes to make sure all were in attendance, Kate called the meeting to order. I glanced around the room—Bill wasn't there and neither was Eric. Jackson wasn't there either. Before I could ask why, Kate answered most of my questions.

"Jackson is helping a former client in Chicago. Eric is showing property and said he would be late. I haven't heard from Detective

Randolph. He set up security, but I don't think he planned to come to the meeting." She looked at Myrtle. "So, let's begin with you."

Myrtle stood up and smoothed her dress. "Maddie, Margaret, and I combined our resources and have food, drink, and decorations under control. Thanks to Max's aunt, we expect this to not only be a memorial to Max but also a lovely garden party that ends with a trip to the third floor for our Scottish Play presentation. Are there any questions?"

Sally Goldman jumped in and reported that she had helped Eric with the donations for the service and the play. "We have more donations in Max's name for the theater. If we ever find a home for our troupe, we should name the place for Max—maybe the Everhart Theater. All of the posters have been distributed for the service and I'm getting responses from a lot of businesses."

Myrtle, Margaret, and Maddie all started talking at once. "Service? What service?"

Kate banged on the table. The hydrangeas swayed, but the vase didn't fall over. I wondered once more if I truly wanted to work for this board—these women never seemed to agree on anything.

Maddie's face was red. "This is a tribute to Mr. Everhart, but no one is going to read the Twenty-third Psalm at *my* garden party."

"It isn't a *funeral*," Myrtle said. "We are celebrating all the wonderful things that he did while he was alive."

"Yes, Max's dearest friend will give a tribute to him. His agent will speak and I will thank the donors," said Kate. "We are the only ones who will speak. Then, when everyone is refreshed, we will go up to the third floor and watch scenes from the…um…Scottish Play. Does anyone have any objections?"

Maxie let out the loudest cat roar I'd ever heard from a kitten and the doorbell rang at the same time. I raced ahead of Aunt Stacy to grab Maxie, but my aunt beat me to the front door. I took Maxie and carried her into the study. After I set her down on the sofa, I looked up.

Aunt Stacy stood in the doorway with a puzzled look on her face. Two strangers were standing beside her. "This is John and Abbie Stewart," she said. "This nice young couple says they have bought my condo and have come to pick up the keys." She cocked her head and looked at me. "I don't remember accepting an offer. I didn't even know that I had an offer on the table."

"Neither did I." I introduced myself to the couple. "We need to find Eric. We need to get this sorted, but I have to go back to my meeting for just a minute."

The couple shook their heads and I tiptoed into the kitchen and over to Kate. "I am excusing myself from this meeting," I whispered. "Matt, Shelia and I will have one more rehearsal before the memorial. That's all I was going to say."

I rejoined Aunt Stacy and the couple and we led them into the living room. "Could we see a copy of your contract? I can't imagine that Eric could sell the condo without my aunt signing a contract."

The couple looked at each other, perplexed, and then back at Aunt Stacy. "He told us that he would contact you," said the man. "We closed on the condo yesterday and he gave us papers with your signature. They're back in our hotel. We just came to get the keys— Mr. Loftis forgot to give them to us."

Abbie, a much younger woman, crossed her legs and settled back in Uncle Hugh's Queen Anne chair. It was obvious, I thought, that she was a trophy wife. "Mr. Loftis was really spry for an old man," she said, "but maybe his memory isn't that great."

I frowned. "Describe him for me."

The Stewarts described the man they'd met with. They agreed that he was an old man with a walking cane and that he had a beard and mustache.

Aunt Stacy and I glanced at each other. This had to be the same old man that had been at the costume shop in Greenville and probably at the Rock House.

"Well," I said, "our real estate agent *isn't* an old man. He's in his late thirties or early forties. He's a partner in Bryant and Loftis Real Estate Company and is young and energetic. We need to find out what's happened here. Give me your contact information and we'll get back to you as soon as we have answers. In the meantime, if I were you, I'd call my bank." I escorted the couple to the front door and watched as they walked to their car and drove away.

I needed to find out if an older gentleman worked for Eric's company, but before I could get to the dining room to retrieve my phone, Bill and his sergeant appeared in the hallway.

"What's going on?" I said.

"I have decided to add more security to the memorial service," he said.

While I retrieved my phone, Aunt Stacy tried to explain to Bill what had just taken place. Before she could finish, Eric rushed into the room, apologizing for being late. He shook his pants legs and dried mud fell onto the floor. "I was showing property at Glassy Mountain and stepped into a mud hole to avoid falling off a ledge." I tried to ignore the amount of mud he had just dropped onto my Persian rug, a rug that might have survived invasions of warriors and probably several wars in the Middle East, and calmed myself. I could vacuum the rug, but I couldn't straighten the mess with the condo without confronting Eric straight on.

"You have some explaining to do," I said. A couple was just here asking for keys to Aunt Stacy's condo, which they reportedly closed on yesterday with an old man from your company. We, of course, didn't give them any keys because Aunt Stacy hasn't signed a contract with you."

Eric blanched. "What? I didn't sell your condo to anyone! Let me see what I can find out," he said. He pulled out his phone and rushed out through the back, leaving another trail of dried mud.

The board meeting was over and members drifted into the living room. Everybody was asking what was happening and it was obvious that Maddie and Myrtle were taking mental notes—juicy tidbits for sharing at their next Junior League meeting. Meanwhile, Aunt Stacy was trying not to cry and I was trying to figure out if our family attorney was up to straightening all of this out.

Bill signaled to me and we went back into the dining room. "I know you have other things on your mind," he said, "but I've discovered that there may be something else hidden in the tunnel that someone is trying to retrieve. *That's* why the chief has ordered it to be completely dug out. There have been a lot of new footprints near the tunnel in the past few days. I have called a forensic technician from Greenville. I came back today to meet the scientist from Tech. We have to get these imprints before they disappear. The footprints from when Max was killed were wiped out before we could get anyone over here to Rosemont."

I was close to hysterical. "Bill, what is going on here? Will I ever have a quiet life in our small southern town? This is more harrowing than living in New York City. I want to sit down in my study and write the play that has been in the back of my head for years. But two people have been murdered, somebody's trying to frighten us away, and now Aunt Stacy's condo may have been stolen out from under her." I could feel tears coming, so I stopped and composed myself. Bill slid his chair next to mine.

"Simmons, we are really close to catching the killer," he whispered. "You can start on the play tomorrow. Just get up, sit down at your desk, and start writing. There is nothing to be afraid of," he said. "But right now, go find where Eric has gotten off to and see about the condo."

All I could think of was a line from Act I, Scene 3 of the Scottish play: *Present fears are less than horrible imaginings.* I was afraid that Aunt Stacy would have to take the Stewarts to court to prove fraud. They'd been in a huff when Aunt Stacy told them the condo wasn't even on the market yet and couldn't be sold. I was afraid that Max and Veronica's killer would come after us while we were sleeping. I had tried to be brave but as Aunt Stacy always said, my patience was wearing thin. I knew I couldn't throw up my hands in defeat—my ancestors refused to *ever* admit defeat.

Eric strode back into the room and plopped into the chair beside Bill. "I don't have a clue about this old man. My Uncle John worked for our company for a while, but he retired and moved to South Florida." He obviously looked at my face. "But don't worry. We will get to the bottom of this. I'm having my assistant check the facts on all our open accounts for the next few days. We will not let anyone sell your condo out from under us. It's obvious someone is trying to make me and my company look like crooks."

"What about the couple?" I said.

"I called them, too. They are getting in touch with their banker to withhold the funds as soon as they get home. Speaking of home, I need to get home and take these nasty clothes off. I'll call you tomorrow." Before anyone could respond, he disappeared through the door.

I turned to Bill. "Is he delusional? How are they going to find the money the Stewarts gave some old man? How did this man even know that Aunt Stacy's condo was for sale? Why would that young couple even think this was legal?"

"Oh, what a tangled web we weave when we practice to deceive." He smiled at me. "But you were already thinking that, weren't you?"

In spite of my anxiety, I giggled. "You know me even better than I thought you did."

"And I hope to know even more—eventually we will have lots of time together, but not right now." He looked away. "My boss cornered me to tell me I can't become involved with anyone that is connected to this case." He looked back at me. "But…I won't always be connected to this case. And that will change soon."

I focused on the last thing he said. "Do you think the killer will be caught soon?"

He nodded and I sighed—his confidence was enough to give me hope that after the memorial for Max, I could help Aunt Stacy settle in and really start writing my play.

We stood up and I walked with him to the front door. I could feel the chemistry between us, but I stepped back when we reached the door. Bill would be the Rosemont chief of police someday and he would be perfect for the job. I wouldn't want to do anything that might jeopardize that. I smiled and closed the door.

Aunt Stacy came charging in from the kitchen. "That nice Stewart man just called. The money from the mortgage company was wired to a bank in the Cayman Islands. I don't know how he got that information but they—and we—have been robbed. How will I be able to help you with the upkeep of this old mansion? I have nowhere else to go. The worst part? The worst part is all the furniture was stolen too, as part of the deal. Great Aunt Ina's secretary is gone forever." Aunt Stacy was dabbing her eyes with a French linen handkerchief.

I patted her on the back. "This wasn't a legal sale and nothing has been stolen. We will sort this all out."

After a brief bite of leftover meeting refreshments, Aunt Stacy went upstairs and I turned off the downstairs lights. I didn't share my real thoughts with her.

All I could think was that "tomorrow and tomorrow" would creep in and the memorial service would be a disaster.

22

The afternoon of the memorial service was, as expected, hot and sunny—but a slight breeze wafted through the garden. I changed clothes three times but finally decided to wear my classic Nicole Miller suit. After all, it was a memorial for Max and not really the garden party that Myrtle and Maddie thought it was.

I checked myself in the antique mirror that stood across from my mahogany dresser. The dresser had been full of scarves, handkerchiefs, and assorted perfume bottles when I'd claimed this as my bedroom. The mirror reflected the image of a woman wearing an elegant navy silk Dupioni suit over an imperial blue silk blouse.

Kate and I had decided to shop in our closets and not buy anything new for the event. Instead, we'd donated the money we saved to the Memorial Fund. The fund had risen beyond our expectations—Eric and his committee had done a fantastic job. I made a mental note to congratulate him on a job well done.

The weather was perfect for an outdoor party. The warmth of summer with an autumn edge to it kept the mosquitoes away. Max's friends and colleagues had come to Rosemont from New York, and the "New York Contingent," as Aunt Stacy called them, were already eating and drinking champagne in the garden. Max's Aunt Mary had also done a great job. She was standing by the tall brick wall at the entrance of the garden greeting people as they walked in.

This has truly turned into a celebration of Max Everhart's life, I thought. A trio from the Rosemont Symphony had donated their time and were playing classical songs as I stepped into the beautiful twilight evening and looked around.

Max would have loved this, I thought. Myrtle, Margaret, and Maddie were holding court with the New York Contingent. Max's agent, his wife, and several producers were laughing and seemed to be having a good time. In spite of the fact that those three women had sometimes been as vocal and obnoxious as Shakespeare's witches, I had to give them a big high-five too for a job well done.

Sally and her husband were lighting the candles on all the tables and helping the caterers bring more food out of the kitchen. Aunt Stacy was giving orders in the kitchen and had it running like a well-oiled machine.

Kate looked stunning in her emerald green dress. She and Jackson were clicking their glasses together. I hoped the toast was to happiness for each other.

I looked around for Bill. With everyone assembled, I felt like we should have an Agatha Christie moment and have him announce the killer and arrest him—or maybe her. But he was holding firm on not spending time with me until Max and Veronica's murders were solved. And although I completely understood, it still made me feel like a suspect. I reminded myself that I wasn't alone—the entire board and even the New York crowd were still suspects too.

I walked around the yard and smiled and spoke to the few people

I knew. I saw Matt, already dressed in his Macbeth robe, go in a side door of the mansion. Their last rehearsal had been perfect—I was sure he and Shelia were going to give a brilliant performance.

I headed toward the closest wine bar beyond the big oak tree. The tree looked almost as sparkly as the stars that were popping out of the night sky. My mind wandered—twilight always reminded me of the times that Michael and I met at our favorite neighborhood bar in New York. After a glass of wine, we would walk hand in hand to our townhouse down the street.

Lost in thought, I tripped over one of the tree's roots and grabbed the arm of a gentleman at the bar. He turned around and I instantly recognized him—Jeff Hill was one of the New York Contingent. He threw his arms around me in a big hug.

"It's great to see you," I said. "I know you and Max were close. How's New York these days?"

"Lonely without you," he said, his eyes twinkling.

Aunt Stacy would say that this man was tall, dark, and handsome. but I didn't agree. Grandmother McBee had always said, "Pretty is as pretty does," and Jeff Hill had never done pretty. I was almost sure that he abused his first wife. I had gone out with him a couple of times but it never led to anything and I was grateful that it hadn't.

Just as he handed me a glass of wine, a big gust of wind blew through the trees. All the candles went out and the hanging lights swayed in the wind. Jeff put his arm around me and was about to force me to kiss him. I started to shove him away when Bill appeared from nowhere. Embarrassed, Jeff jumped back like he had been burned. I acted as if nothing had happened. "It was nice to see you, Jeff," I said. "I'm glad that you could come for the memorial."

I grabbed Bill's arm and pulled him toward the house. "That was a great save," I said. "Jeff could be Max and Veronica's killer. He wasn't one of my favorite producers in New York and he and Max disagreed on almost every project they worked on together." I glanced around. Something about that wind gave me déjà vu. It was like we were reliving our first board meeting when Max was stabbed. I took a deep breath and changed the subject. "Is everything running smoothly behind the scenes? Have you had any security problems?"

Bill scanned the garden and, intentionally not looking at me, whispered, "Simmons, I'm almost sure that the killer is here tonight. I have extra security—a lot of the cops are dressed like guests."

He paused. "Be careful. Do NOT go somewhere by yourself tonight. The killer has either been targeting you or, indirectly, the mansion, which involves you. Max lost a lot of money—a lot of people's money. This began years ago about the time the Rosemont theater group started going to New York every year for plays and shopping—back, when you were still there, when they came to see you at the Forty-Second Street Theater. There's no telling whose money he lost."

"But what does that have to do with me?"

"Well, for one thing, the exact amount that the Stewart couple say they paid for your Aunt Stacy's condo went first to a New York account associated with Max. We're still trying to trace it." He looked at me and frowned. "I haven't seen anyone who looks like the old man you and others have described, but I know he is here, Simmons. You are not safe. Promise me that you will not be alone—even if you go to the ladies' room—at any time tonight. Always stay with the crowd. And make sure your aunt isn't alone either."

Before I could respond, he moved toward the house. Jeff was gone, so I turned back toward the bar. One of Aunt Stacy's dearest friends, dressed in black with opera length pearls hanging around her neck, came up beside me and told me the memorial service had been wonderful. Several other people joined her, and I slipped away into the crowd toward the front of the outdoor stage.

The wind had died down. All the candles had been relit and the fairy lights were twinkling in the trees, and I breathed a sigh of relief.

Kate stepped up to the podium and banged her gavel and I smiled to myself. She liked banging that gavel and she could bang all she wanted tonight because it wasn't on my antique dining room table. The crowd got quiet and she welcomed the guests and introduced the members of the board.

I headed to the kitchen to check on Aunt Stacy and the caterers. She had covered her black dress with an apron that had the British crown on it. "It's from Buckingham Palace," she said. It was one of the many souvenirs from her extensive travels.

There were charcuterie boards, trays of cucumber sandwiches surrounded by cucumber roses, and numerous other mouthwatering plates. Later, after the last guest had finally left, I was going to sneak into the kitchen, get a plate from the cabinet, and fill it up with some of everything. "Aunt Stacy, the food all looks and smells divine."

"Don't thank *me*," she said. "Max's Aunt Mary ordered all his favorite foods. Southern Caterers has done an exceptional job. We are having a great time. The next time we have a party, I plan to hire this company."

I heard Kate say something about Max's agent and I placed my finger on my lips. "Kate is introducing the speaker. I want to hear this." I hurried back outside and slid up next to Max's aunt. I could tell that she was holding back tears and I reached for her hand. Max would have been pleased—all the praise would have fed his hefty ego. I wondered if Veronica were alive if she would have regretted leaving him.

Bill was obviously disappointed that the killer hadn't been caught before the memorial and I was too. I figured that after tonight, it might be forever before we knew the who, what, and why of the murders.

At the end of Max's agent's tribute, Kate stepped back up to the microphone and invited everyone to follow her up the back steps to the third floor. As our guests meandered after her, I started blowing out candles.

I had walked around a corner to snuff out candles in a side yard when suddenly I realized I had done exactly what Bill had warned me about—I was alone in a forest of darkness. I turned back toward the garden and saw a movement, the shadow of a dim figure coming my way. When I rounded the corner back toward the lights, I saw that the figure coming toward me was Matt—I recognized the robe.

Oh, no, I thought. What was he doing there? "Matt? What's wrong? You should already be upstairs. Is someone hurt?"

He grabbed my arm and jerked me around to face him and I saw that it wasn't Matt at all. I found myself staring into the crazed blue eyes of Eric Loftis.

23

Eric grabbed the sleeve of my jacket and jerked me forward and one of my Monolo Blahnik shoes shot in the air and landed on a pile of dirt in front of the tunnel. The other fell off as he dragged me along. Oh, well, I thought. At least Kate would recognize that they were my shoes.

"Hurry up," he said. "You're going in the tunnel before anyone sees us. I have to make an appearance upstairs and I don't want anyone to get suspicious."

"The tunnel?" I screeched. "I'll suffocate in there."

"Yes, I know," he growled. "I had planned to stab you like I did Max, but it doesn't matter how you die as long as you're out of my way. I thought when I first met you that we could work well as a couple. But then you started chasing that loser Bill Randolph."

He shoved me into the tunnel into an area that was more like a cave. He must've dug out the room I thought I'd seen that first day. So *that's* where the mud on his shoes had come from.

I couldn't believe it—this man had had the nerve to sit down with Aunt Stacy and me and eat our food when all the while he was planning to kill me.

I fell into empty darkness and that familiar musky smell permeated my nostrils. Now it all made sense—it was Eric's after-shave!

"Please. Stop. I have done nothing to you," I said. "Why are you doing this? Are you crazy?"

I felt the sting of his hand on my face and blood coming out of my nose. I tried to sniff but he slapped me again, harder this time, and I crumpled against a wall.

"I am going to tie you up. I'll make my appearance upstairs and then come back to deal with you."

"Why are you doing this?" I asked again.

His eyes were like ice. "McBee Mansion should be mine," he said through clenched teeth. "Your great-uncle stole this house from my family."

I said nothing and he continued. "My uncle, Alfred Redfern, played poker every Thursday night with him and a well-known group at the mansion. One night, the group said my uncle owed too much money and couldn't play anymore until he covered all his debt. It was a lie—it was *your* great-uncle who owed the money. He should have given the mansion to my family to cover *his* debts. Your uncle cheated my family—this mansion belongs to me!"

I tried to kick him but missed and blood, still pouring from my nose, spattered across his shirt. Wielding a chef's knife I recognized from the kitchen, he slit the front of my blouse, and I began to sob. Someone should have missed us by now, I thought, but there was no one.

Eric stood over me, still raving. "You were spying on me when you showed up at the pharmacy with your Aunt Stacy. I knew then that you had found out I was bipolar and that would ruin everything. You were on to me and I had to stop you. I thought pushing your aunt down the library steps would've stopped her."

I finally found my voice. "But, why Max?"

"I lost a lot of money at the Borgata Casino and Max paid off my debts. When I gave him some money toward paying off my debts, he used it as an investment in a Ponzi scheme. But that's not all—he opened the account in my name, so when he lost all the money, it looked like it was me who had cooked up the whole thing. So when the FBI found out about it, I would be the one who went to jail, not him!"

His face was now red with rage. I tried to move but he grabbed a chair from somewhere—one of the Windsor chairs I had planned to replace—and slammed me into it. Once my hands and feet were secured, he picked up the knife he'd slit my blouse with and came toward me.

I had to buy some time. "How did you even *know* Max?"

He sneered. "Don't pretend that you don't remember. I studied at the American Musical and Dramatic Academy in New York City and auditioned for the role of Macbeth—I was great for the role—and he didn't give it to me. You could've helped me, but you did nothing. I could have had a career in the theater except for you and Max. I didn't have the money to pay for the next year of school. That's when I came back home and got my real estate license.

"Then, when I got elected to the Rhett Street Players board, I was excited. I knew I had a chance to restart my career. And then, who did they hire as the new director? You." He raised the knife and then glanced at his watch and lowered it. "I would stab you now, but

I want to watch you die. I'll do it when I get back from upstairs. I've got to get up there and prove just how good I am."

He was staring off in space, reliving his past. I tried to figure out how to get myself untied but I had to be subtle and careful. *Things done well and with care exempt themselves from fear*, I thought.

"Wait! You *are* good, Eric. You were the old man weren't you—the one who sold Aunt Stacy's condo."

His face lit up. "Clever, wasn't it? I invented him as my alter ego. I dressed up like my Uncle Alfred—the would-be Lord of McBee Mansion. He could do things that I couldn't do. It also gave me some acting practice to help my career. I was convincing, wasn't I?"

"Did you kill Veronica too?"

"Oh, yeah. But she was much harder to kill than Max. I had to hold her under the water for a long time."

"But why did you kill her? Her Aunt Mary said she was leaving Max."

"Exactly. She had agreed to meet me on her way back from Highlands. I was going to make her give me money, but she said that she didn't have any. She lied and said she'd had to take a second-rate part in a movie to help Max pay off his debts to his aunt."

I breathed as slowly as I could although my heart was about to beat out of my chest. "Eric, you should go upstairs now. You don't want anyone to remember later that you weren't there."

"You're right," he said. Finally, he nodded and disappeared. As soon as I was sure he was gone, I rocked the Windsor chair back and forth and finally felt the back pull away from the seat. The wooden dowels loosened and the chair and I collapsed into a heap, but my hands were free!

I held my breath to listen for an indication that someone else was around. Had no one missed me? Would anyone think to look for me in the tunnel?

Stay focused, I told myself. I had to get out of the tunnel before Eric returned. I untied my ankles and tried to stand up but my knees buckled, so I crawled instead through piles of dirt toward the entrance.

Twinkling lights from the garden trees came into view and I managed to get to a table. Trying to pull myself up, I missed and grabbed the tablecloth, and the punch bowl and cups came crashing down around me.

Within seconds I heard a comotion. Bill was the first to get to me and I motioned for him to lean down. "It's Eric!" I yelled as loud as I could. "Eric Loftis is the killer!" I heard my words echo across the garden.

Now in a suit, Eric jumped the last of the back steps and sprinted for the trees. Bill yelled to one of his officers to call an ambulance for me and took off after Eric.

Aunt Stacy appeared from nowhere and gently dabbed around my nose, which had started to bleed again. "It's all going to be okay, Simmons," she said. "An ambulance is on the way."

"All's well that ends well," I said, nodding.

And with that, I passed out cold.

24

I opened my eyes and tried to turn my head but quickly stopped. My nose throbbed and I hurt all over.

"She's awake!" someone said and I recognized Aunt Stacy's voice. A nurse hurried in and took my blood pressure.

"What happened?" I said. "Am I okay?"

Aunt Stacy took my hand and squeezed lightly. "Yes, you're okay, but you are lucky to be alive. You have a broken nose, a couple of broken ribs, and a broken arm—and your suit and blouse have been trashed. Oh, and you also have a mild concussion." Tears streamed down her wrinkled cheeks.

I glanced down and realized I had on one of those gaping hospital gowns. "Definitely not designed by Ralph Lauren," I said.

"Kate will be here to sit with you in a few minutes and I will go home and get clean nightgowns for you," said my aunt. I didn't have the heart to tell Aunt Stacy that I don't sleep in a nightgown—or anything. It would be too much information for her.

I looked around to see exactly where I was—it was a typical hospital room with a clean and sterile environment. I'd been in a room like this one before—my mother had spent years at this hospital as a volunteer. I relaxed—glad that I had landed in a safe place where staff knew my family. Rosemont Medical Center was the best in the area.

The door creaked and turned my head to see Kate carrying a huge pot filled with a miniature gardenia bush. Aunt Stacy said her goodbyes and Kate set the flower pot on a table near the window.

"Thank goodness you are alive," she said. "And I've got to say you certainly know how to give a memorial service a whiz-bang finish. You'll be the talk of Rosemont and the New York City theater district for years to come."

I tried to laugh but my ribs hurt. "Did they catch Eric?"

"Not yet," said Kate. "As soon as you screamed that Eric was the killer, everybody started running after him. Bill chased him all the way to the Reedy River but lost him there. A huge crowd on the Freedom Bridge watched him swim downriver and disappear.

"Bill said to tell you he will come to the hospital later to tell you more and interview you. He's hoping Eric said something specific to you about his plans. They found an airline ticket to the Cayman Islands—he dropped it while running. The state law enforcement guys and the FBI have also gotten involved. There's a statewide search for him."

She reached to give me a hug and then thought better of it and just patted my hand. "Take it easy for the next couple of days. We will have a meeting of the board and do a recap of the memorial service next week." I nodded and she smiled. "Simms, your Aunt Stacy is so proud of you. You saved yourself and you saved the day for all of us."

That would be all I heard—the medication they'd given me had taken effect and I drifted away.

The next morning, I awoke with a start, my heart slamming in my chest. A shadow appeared at the door and crossed the room and I screamed.

"It's okay," said a young woman. "I'm Angie." She flipped on the lights and wrote the date and her name on the whiteboard next to the television. "The doctor says that if your vital signs are okay, you are going home this morning." She took my blood pressure and looked at the pupils in my eyes. "All looks good," she said. "I will change your bandages and we'll get the discharge papers signed. And I'll be back to get you ready."

More than two hours passed before Angie finally helped me into a wheelchair and pushed me to sliding doors to the outside where Aunt Stacy was waiting with her car. There was a slight drizzle, but I managed to get myself into the front seat.

Aunt Stacy patted me on the leg. "Maxie is waiting for you and she's been crying for you nonstop. She—and I—are both happy that you are coming home."

"That Maxie," I said. "She knew Eric Loftis was bad news from the start. I should have paid attention to her."

Aunt Stacy nodded. "I made spaghetti for lunch. I know it is your favorite comfort food." She paused. "I have medication from the hospital pharmacy and will give you a dose when we get home. And, I put clean sheets on your bed so you can rest for the next few days."

Joan was waiting for us when we pulled up to the mansion. Together, she and Aunt Stacy somehow got me into bed. I have such wonderful friends, I thought, as I drifted, once again, to sleep.

25

When I next opened my eyes, it was dark outside and rainy. I looked around the room and realized I was safely in my bed back at home. I tried to sit up but pain shot through my ribs. Maxie stretched and moved to the foot of my bed.

Just then, I heard a scratching noise at the window. A branch is probably rubbing against it, I thought. I turned over to try and get a better look. Then, suddenly, a form appeared from behind the drapes. A man lunged toward the bed and covered my mouth with one hand. Although he wore a mask, I knew who it was.

"Thanks to you, the FBI has frozen all my accounts," said Eric. "I can't leave until I have my money so you're going to give it to me. Simmons, I will kill you if you don't hand it over right now."

I murmured and he removed his hand from my mouth. "And don't scream or I'll stab you right now." I glanced at his other hand. In it was a dagger like the one he'd killed Max with.

"Okay," I said. I pushed myself away from the pillows with my unbroken arm and reached over to the table beside the bed. "My checkbook is in here. Let me get it." Instead of reaching for the drawer, of course, I grabbed the Bradley Hubbard brass lamp that had been on the bedside table for years. Just then, Maxie leaped and dug her claws into his back, and I swung the lamp as hard as I could at his head. Eric sprawled against the curtains, stabbing at Maxie to try and get her off of him. But before he could right himself, the bedroom door swung open.

Aunt Stacy stood in the doorway, holding Uncle Hugh's 1873 Winchester shotgun at eye level. "Eric Loftis, put that knife down and your hands up or I will blow your head off."

Even in his crazed state, I think he knew she was serious—and did as he was told. Sirens wailed and within seconds, Bill, a SLED agent and two men from the FBI were standing at the foot of my bed. I pulled the sheet up around my body and Maxie began to clean her claws.

Bill handcuffed Eric and handed him off to the SLED agent, pointing at my attacker's head. "He'll probably need stitches for that cut," he said. We all watched as he was removed from the room.

I focused my eyes and looked at Bill. "Did I hurt him?"

He laughed. "Between you and Maxie and Annie Oakley here, I'd say so."

Aunt Stacy lowered the shotgun and leaned it by the door. "Glad he believed me. I've been meaning to pick up some shells for this old thing but hadn't gotten around to it." All three of us laughed till we cried and the pain in my ribs was worth it.

When I finally composed myself, I looked at Bill. "How did you get here so fast?" He pointed at Aunt Stacy.

"I called him before I got the gun," she said.

At that, real tears ran down my cheeks and she sat on the bed and gently put her arms around me.

"Oh, Simmons, I'm sorry," she said.

I heard MacBeth's dying words in my head. *It is too late. He drags me down; I sink, I sink.*

"Bill, do you think this is the end? Are we finally safe?"

He wrapped his arms around both me and Aunt Stacy. "You have never been safer," he said. "I'll make sure of it. And yes, it's over. Eric Loftis will not hurt you—or anyone else—again."

Maxie squirmed in between us all and purred her agreement.

26

The sound of Kate's gavel against my antique dining table brought the Rhett Street Players meeting to order. It had been almost a month since Max's memorial, my nose had mostly healed, and my tennis game seemed to be better since my wrist and ribs had mended.

"Quiet, everyone, please." Kate banged the gavel again. "We are here today to vote on a major issue for our troupe. We've all done our research and looked at every angle of this offer. I'm going to repeat the details. It needs to be clear to all of us what our commitment will be."

She cleared her throat. "We have found a home and will use McBee Mansion only as a rehearsal hall. Our new home will be in an old cotton warehouse in the West Village of Rosemont. The west end of Rosemont is waking up to new growth. Art galleries and restaurants have implemented the vision of our city council. We are fortunate that the Ferridays—who own the warehouse— are philanthropic and want to donate part of the building to the Rhett Street Players. The money we made from Max's memorial will cover most of the rest of the asking price. Jackson, our treasurer, says that this is doable."

She looked around the room. "Are there any questions? No? Then would a board member propose a motion that this be accepted?"

Myrtle Myers jumped up. "I move that we accept the donation and use the money from Max's memorial to pay everything else."

Sally answered with a second, and we all jumped up when Kate asked for a vote. "Aye," we yelled in unison and the motion carried. Hugs were given and received all around.

"This is a truly historic day," said Kate. "Finally, we have a place to work and promote theater. Now, let's have a glass of wine and toast the new Everhart Theater of Rosemont."

Aunt Stacy came from the kitchen with a tray full of appetizers. Maddie was right behind her with another tray loaded with wine and glasses. We all helped ourselves.

Bill entered the room from the hall with Maxie snuggled against his chest. She was purring so loud we could all hear her. "Could I have everyone's attention?" he said.

Everyone quieted again. "I wanted all of you to know that Eric Loftis was indicted by a grand jury this morning on more counts than I can name. He's been charged and arraigned, and his bail is set for over a million dollars. Given the evidence we have and Simmons's testimony, it is unlikely that he'll ever return to Rosemont as a free man." A large cheer rose from all the board members and Aunt Stacy and I hugged each other.

We celebrated together for another hour and then one by one, the board members departed. I had not seen much of Bill in the past few weeks as he had been helping the FBI prepare the case against Eric. It was hot and still light outside, so we decided to walk down to the river. He took my hand, and we strolled silently along the riverbank. I could hear the falls in the distance as we approached Main Street.

"I bet I can guess what's running through your mind," Bill said. He scooped up a rock and skipped it across the water.

"What?"

"All's well that ends well."

"Wrong."

The falls from the river cascaded across the rocks and splashed onto the bank—and my shoes. I scooted away straight into Bill's arms and he cocked his head at me. "What *were* you thinking, then?"

"Neither a borrower nor a lender be."

"That's from *Hamlet*, isn't it?"

"Yes," I said. "I've been thinking it's time we focused on a different play."

"Good idea," he said, as our lips finally met.

Acknowledgments

First, I would like to acknowledge the support of my dear family, friends, and the Lexi Lamda Chis. B.J. Koonce gave me the inspiration for *Murder Strikes the Set* with her Thursday Club paper, "The Scottish Play."

Many thanks to the Upstate South Carolina chapter of Sisters In Crime and to all my other readers.

Debbie Hudson is the greatest typist ever. Vally Sharpe was the perfect editor for Simmons and Rosemont.